"Why Me?" I Asked Myself.

But it had been a "why me?" day, I swear. At lunch the Morgan Monsters, the most popular boys' club in the Morgan School, accidentally published their secret list of best girls. Actually someone stole it, had it typed and mimeographed, and then sold it. It cost me fifty cents to read about the girl with the best personality, the best smile, the best body, the best all-around sex appeal, the most likely to succeed, the most kissable, and on and on until it made me sick to my stomach. I wasn't anywhere on the MM list. My sister, Abigail, was. She got it for Best Brain.

But my real problem is that I'm a middle child, sandwiched between two geniuses. How can I be special, too? I'm nearly twelve and *something* has to change—soon!

The Middle of the Sandwich is the Best Part

Judi Miller

A MINSTREL® BOOK

PUBLISHED BY POCKET BOOKS

New York   London   Toronto   Sydney   Tokyo   Singapore

A MINSTREL PAPERBACK *ORIGINAL*

A Minstrel Book published by
POCKET BOOKS, a division of Simon & Schuster Inc.
1230 Avenue of the Americas, New York, NY 10020

ISBN: 0-671-66575-8

First Minstrel Books printing September 1990

10 9 8 7 6 5 4 3 2 1

A MINSTREL BOOK and colophon are registered trademarks of
Simon & Schuster Inc.

Printed in the U.S.A.

For all middle children everywhere

The Middle of the Sandwich is the Best Part

"Hey, little girl, your shoelaces are untied," the man sitting near the front of the bus said.

See, that kind of thing throws me. I hate, first of all, being addressed as "hey, little girl." It's that I feel the person saying it is insulting me. So I tripped over my untied shoelace and slid to the bottom of the steps and halfway out the door into the pouring rain. I also hate to be told my shoelaces are untied.

"Herman, wait!" I yelled.

Herman was the name I had given to my umbrella, a legend in its lifetime until that day. I had had it for thirteen months, but now it had opened itself inside out and was flying down a long street in New York City called West End Avenue.

I could only see a flash of orange silk as it rolled away

on its spokes. No doubt about it, Herman was dying, and I had to get off the bus and run home in the pouring rain.

Already the bus driver was shouting, "Okay, move it along. Little girl, get your hand out of the door unless you want to leave it behind."

"Bye," some people on the bus said.

So there I stood in a rain that felt like a water bed turned upside down and emptied, and I knew it was hopeless to look for Herman, who would now be useless. I said a silent prayer for him and started to run, sloshing in my shoes through a puddle that looked like a small pond.

I slung my book bag over my shoulder. I could feel my navy blazer, plaid pleated skirt, white knee socks, and white blouse sticking to me like a wet bathing suit. It felt as if my hair had just been washed without my special seaweed shampoo, and my shoes were making squishing sounds like little tubs full of water, which they were. I had just four blocks to run from the bus stop to the front of my apartment building, but right then they seemed like four miles.

"Why me?" I asked myself. That was my favorite question. There was never an answer for it.

The whole day had been a Why Me day, I swear. The Morgan Monsters—the most popular boys' club in my school, Morgan—had had a secret list of theirs stolen.

It was stolen by another boys' club and Xeroxed. It had cost me fifty cents to buy it and read who was the most popular girl, the girl with the nicest smile, the girl with the best body, the sweetest girl, and on and on until I felt sick to my stomach. I wasn't anywhere on the MM list. My sister Abigail was. She got it for Best Brain. Lucky her.

I took a giant leap over a tiny reservoir and landed on the curb, splashing myself anyway. I would never make their stupid list for best athlete, that was for sure. Biggest klutz, I might have had a chance.

See, eleven is a nothing age. They say it's too old for dolls, but I still play with my Barbies. I'm also too young for boys. But the real problem is that none of the boys I like, like me. I also have another problem. I'm a middle child. "So what?" you might say. But as anyone will tell you, middle children have problems. My problem is my older sister Abigail, who has never made a grade less than an A in her entire life. As a matter of fact, she was included in an article in the *Daily News* about super-bright children. She was the only girl with an unbroken all-A and sometimes A+ record. My parents had it laminated so it hangs in her room with her name circled in red. Abbie isn't bad looking, either, though I hate to admit it. She has longish taffy-colored hair and blue-green eyes and is tall and slim.

As if that wouldn't be bad enough, there's my younger brother, Christopher, who's going on ten. My mom figured the easiest way to name her kids was to do it in alphabetical order. I don't think she's planning on a D, though, so I'm stuck in the middle. Anyway, when Chris was just three years old we went over to my aunt Molly's apartment in Greenwich Village. Chris reached up with his little fingers and started to play a tune that sounded like "Jingle Bells" or something. It sounded really great when my aunt found a chair for him and put cushions on it. Then my mom's mission in life became to find a piano teacher for Chris. He was only three, remember!

We got a secondhand piano and were all supposed to take lessons, but I didn't like it, and Abbie had too much homework to do to practice. Finally, when Chris was five, he and his piano teacher, Carl von Lutz (we call him Lutzy; I privately call him Klutzy), shopped around for a baby grand piano. My almost-ten-year-old brother is a musical genius, a child prodigy. At eight-going-on-nine he gave his first concert (he had graduated from recitals at age six). It was at Town Hall, and Chris, wearing a tiny tuxedo and looking like a large penguin, wowed them. He had his review from the *New York Times* laminated. It is hanging in his room.

I have a calendar hanging in my room.

No wonder I didn't make the Morgan Monsters list for being anything special. I wasn't.

But not for long. I made up my mind that twelve

would be better than eleven. I even had a plan. I have lots of plans.

I thought of that as I tore through the rain without Herman. It still hurt to think of him skidding away somewhere. He was more than an umbrella. More like a friend I could talk to in the rain. Finally I squeaked and squished my way to the lobby of my apartment building, where I stood dripping on the red carpet. The doorman looked at me sympathetically, and I tried to smile. Wouldn't you know it? As soon as I got into the lobby the rain stopped and the sun peeped through the clouds. Can I call them right? Wouldn't you know it on a Why Me day?

The doorman dug into his pocket and handed me a note. I knew right away from the lavender-smelling paper it could only be from my grandma. She has an apartment in the building, too. But it's down the hall and in another wing. She's one of my best friends.

After wringing out my skirt I took the note and listened to my shoes and socks squish as I made my way to the elevator.

I waited until I got to our apartment door to open her note, which was folded into a teeny piece of paper. Grandma had this thing about not wanting to impose on us. We also didn't want to impose on her, so we hardly ever saw her. Except for me. Like I said, she and I were the best of friends.

Betsi, darling,

   You should stop up soon. Have I got a cream rinse for you! Though personally, I like your hair curly. People pay good money to get it to look that way.

Grandma loves you

   Getting a note from Grandma was like getting a birthday card.

   I couldn't wait to get out of my wet clothes, so I quietly let myself into the apartment. Chris was practicing and almost drowned out my squishing shoes. Our apartment opens onto a long hallway with rooms off it. I could hear my fourteen-year-old sister Abigail whining to my mom in the kitchen. I got into my room and changed into jeans, then I went back toward the kitchen, hoping to use the phone.

   Just my luck. Abbie and my mom were still in there having one of their heavy discussions.

   "Mother," Abbie said in that snooty way I hated, "all the girls are going to the movie. It's about this woman who did all these great things, and it's for a school project."

   That was how Abbie always got her way. It was always for a school project. Chris always had a concerto he wanted to hear. Me? Nothing. No one even had time to ask about me.

I could see my mom was trying to work. She's a free-lance copywriter. She's the one who comes up with all the clever sayings and slogans and words under an ad, and also the headline of the ad. She's really good, too. A lot of her stuff appears in magazines and newspapers, and sometimes she writes radio commercials, too. She doesn't work in an office because of us three kids.

"But, Abigail, dear, that's an R-rated movie. Surely your teacher doesn't want you girls seeing that." I could tell Abbie would win. It was just a matter of minutes. My mom was too busy to fight any longer.

"*Mother*, I wasn't born yesterday," Abbie said, holding to her position, which was probably that it was a semi-smutty movie, but she could use it anyway.

I looked at my mom. She always looked great. Her eyes sparkled, and she had my hair, only the way I wanted it on myself. It was straight but orange like mine. She wore funny T-shirts with cute sayings, and when she was writing she wore a baseball cap turned sideways. It was on sideways then. I knew I would have the kitchen alone soon.

She finally relented and asked Abbie to bring her bag from the living room. Abbie would get to go. I knew it, and so did she.

"Get caught in the rain, sweetheart?" my mom said. I shrugged. I needed to make a very private phone call. In the bottom drawer of my dresser was the reason.

There was a copy of *Backstage*, which is a paper that tells about acting jobs. The one I wanted to call about said, "Child Models Wanted—no experience necessary."

If I could just get a modeling job before I was twelve, that would do it for me. I would be special—a child model. Not just a nothing sandwiched between two gifted children. This was my chance. The article said they were looking for wholesome, natural-looking kids. That was me.

As soon as everyone left the kitchen my hand was on the phone as if it were a hot line. Lisa and Lida, the twins, my friends from school, said they wanted to find out about becoming models, too. Frantically I dialed their number. What if they forgot? What if they chickened out? What would I do if they decided not to go?

We had three other sets of twins at my school, but none of them were identical like Lisa and Lida. You literally couldn't tell them apart by looking at them. They both had long, straight blond hair and were very cute and petite. They'd be knockouts when they became teenagers for real.

On the phone you could tell the difference easily, though. Lida had this husky, low voice, and Lisa had a high, squeaky voice.

Lida answered on the first ring. They were waiting for me to call. I could hear Lisa breathing on an extension phone.

"We don't know if we should go. My mom would kill us," Lida said.

"So you don't have to tell her everything," I said.

"That would be a lie," Lida said, outraged.

Then Lisa piped in, "No, it isn't. She didn't ask, so it's not a lie."

"It's dangerous on Times Square," Lida protested, knowing she was going to lose the fight. I knew all about Lida. She wanted to go to see about modeling, but she was afraid they would choose Lisa and not her.

Finally it was decided—we were going. Lisa and Lida had stepped away from the phone to have a loud argument. When they came back Lisa, her voice higher and squeakier than ever, announced, "Okay, we'll meet you by the Ninety-sixth Street subway stop on Broadway." I could walk it in seven and a half minutes. We decided to dress a little younger. Maybe an Alice-in-Wonderland look.

I decided on my red velveteen jumper, a frilly white blouse, a red-and-white headband, white socks, and my patent leather Mary Janes that I hadn't even worn in a year. I studied the effect in the mirror. I would definitely be special before I was twelve.

I had just five minutes to write in my diary. I knew that the next time I wrote in it I would be a child model, and then probably a child star.

Dear Diary,

Diary, there are just eleven days to go until I am twelve. This is Day One. I'm going to be something special. A model. Abbie couldn't do it because she disagrees with modeling. She feels it isn't good for a girl to act like a store dummy. Chris couldn't do it, either, because it takes him all day just to get into his little tuxedo.

I'm going with L and L. Just think, DD, when I write next, I'll be SOMEBODY.

Today in the hall, by my locker, Donny came over. He looked at me, smiled, and said, "Hi, Betsi." I figured he had decided to run for class president. My knees felt weak, and my throat was so dry I couldn't swallow. So I didn't say anything. Just remembered to smile a little. At this rate I'll never get anywhere. Every girl in the school likes him. He's got jet-black curly hair and a beautiful face with an athletic body. Chalk up another one for me. He comes down the hall and I can't even say, "Hi!"

Well, DD, wish me luck!

Today was a kind of a lime-green day. But it looks like it might be bright and shiny green with gold stripes soon. One bad thing, I didn't make the Morgan Monsters slam book, which had the girls they were interested in. I guess they don't know I exist. I guess I'd give a C- to today so

10

far. If the interview turns out A+, I'll change the day's grade to a B.

Love and xxx's
Betsi with an *i*

I put my diary in its usual hiding place in my drawer. My drawers are always a mess, so no one would even know it was there. My grandmother gave it to me last Christmas. It's powder blue with a gold ribbon for a marker, and it matches my all-powder-blue room. I'm always forgetting to write in it because nothing special ever happens to me. But I vowed to write every day from now on, because when I'm rich and famous, people will probably want to read it.

I sneaked quietly down the front hall to the door. Chris and Lutzy were still talking about his lesson. Abbie was probably munching popcorn all alone in a dark theater watching a movie my mother would blush to see. And I—I was on my way to becoming a kid model.

The elevator was empty as I went down. The doorman tipped his hat to me, I guess because I was all dressed up. The sun was shining, and it was as if it hadn't rained at all. I began to run up West End Avenue and turned toward Broadway, where the twins were going to be waiting in front of the subway station.

As I got nearer I could see that they weren't there

yet. Only two blond girls who looked like teenagers were standing there. They were dressed alike. Black leather pants, jackets to match, and black leather caps. Boy, was I dense. That was the twins! They had changed their minds. I thought I was going to be the first eleven-going-on-twelve-year-old to have a massive coronary right on Ninety-sixth Street and Broadway.

"How could you do this to me?" I yelled at them as I got closer. Great. Alice in Wonderland and twins wearing what models were supposed to wear. Fat chance I'd have sitting next to them!

"We changed our minds, but it was too late to call you," Lisa said.

"You look really great," Lida said.

"But . . ." I protested. It was too late. We had to apply to be models from four to six. It was four-fifteen, and it was too late to change. We linked arms and went into the subway station. I was very quiet on the subway. Usually I don't talk because I have to shout over the roar of the train. But I wasn't talking then because I felt I looked funny. I had lost my confidence, which wasn't one of my strong points anyway.

Finally we pushed off the subway car, fighting the herds of people trying to get on. Breathless, I looked around me. I smelled hot dogs and fried doughnuts, but I told myself that as a model I wouldn't be able to eat everything I wanted. That would be the bad part, but it was better to be special, so I decided to trade hot dogs for fame.

When we climbed out of the subway station we landed right in the middle of Times Square. My mom was worried about precious Abigail going to see an R-rated movie. I wondered how she'd feel about me in the X-rated part of the city. I didn't think my mom would be too thrilled about my being there.

We passed the sleazy movie theaters and concentrated on walking toward Fifth Avenue near the main public library. On Fifth Avenue we came to a really snazzy-looking building.

"That's the wrong address," Lisa said as we started to go in. We went next door to a not-so-nice building that must have been in the process of being remodeled.

As we approached the elevator a man with a shabby uniform said, "You must be going to Kiddie Shots." He said it as if he was proud of himself.

"It's on the sixth floor," Lisa and Lida said together.

"It's on the sixth floor," he said as if he had said it first.

I was chewing gum to calm my nerves, but I had gotten to the stage where I cracked it every five seconds. Lida looked at me and shook her head. I took the gum out of my mouth but didn't know where to stick it. I just stuck it onto the elevator door as we got out. I felt more nervous than ever.

There was a hall full of offices. The door we wanted

had bumpy glass on it, and one of the *D*s in Kiddie Shot was turning sideways, falling off. We opened the door, and all three of us tried to get in at once. Lisa and Lida were giggling. I felt scared to death. I had to become a model. I just had to. With that thought, my Mary Jane shoes slid on the carpet, and I lost my balance and stumbled toward the receptionist's desk, finally stopping when I sprawled across the top of it.

"Yeeeess," she said sweetly, ignoring the fact that my head was almost on her shoulder.

While I was stammering my name Lisa and Lida gave theirs out crystal clear.

"Twiiiiins," she said, smiling. "We just love twins!"

She had glasses that slipped on her nose and a wild, frizzy hairdo, and one of her two front teeth was chipped.

She handed us forms to fill out and pointed to some chairs that were unoccupied. The room was packed with kids of every size, shape, and color. All of them had one thing in common—loud voices. We were the only ones who had come without our mothers. If we'd had to bring them, we wouldn't have been there at all.

"What should we say our ages are?" Lisa asked.

"Fourteen," I said.

"Try twelve," Lida said. "That's what we are. Almost. They'll know."

Surprisingly we were the first to be called into the inner-inner office. "You three can go in to see Ms.

Ida,'' the receptionist said, and some of the mothers with screaming kids scowled at her. I stood up between the twins and immediately sank to the ground on rubbery feet. One of my feet had fallen asleep, but I was too numb to notice. They each grabbed an arm so I didn't fall flat on my face.

"Betsi, are you okay?" Lisa whispered.

I brushed the lint off my jumper, stood upright, and said, "I never felt better."

"Well, you're acting kind of weird," Lida hissed.

Chapter

TWO

"Twins," Ms. Ida cooed. "I just love twins."

I felt my heart slipping down to my shoes. In front of us was a lady with bright yellow hair, bright purple-red lipstick that went higher than her lipline, a small square hat, and a cigarette in her mouth. She continuously smoked cigarettes.

"Twins sell soft drinks, gum, candy. How old are you two darling creatures?"

"Fourteen," said Lisa.

"Eleven," said Lida.

Then they gave each other a dirty look.

"And what does this one do?" she asked, swiveling in her chair to face me.

"I'm going to be fourteen, and I want to be a model."

She smiled and seemed to like what I had said. Then

she put another cigarette in a long holder and said, "We are looking for child models. New faces. Always looking for new types." For a second her face disappeared behind a cloud of smoke.

I stole a look at Lisa and Lida as they sneaked a peek at me. Then we turned to Ms. Ida.

She pounded her fist on the desktop, and some papers hopped around. "There are jobs, many jobs," she told us firmly, and then she realigned the pile of paper. Her fingernails were very long and very red like her hat, sweater, and lipstick. "You just have to work hard! Are you ready to work hard?"

We all nodded as if our heads were being pulled by marionette strings. She reached for the phone and dialed. "Bud?" She covered the receiver with her snazzy red fingernails and whispered to us, "Bud is the art director at *Seventeen* magazine."

Then she went back to the phone.

"Yes, Bud. I think I have just what you're looking for. Twins. Blond. They look like sleek cats, and I have this girl with squiggly orangish hair, and she's as cute as a Muppet."

I felt my face getting red. I was a Muppet while they were sleek cats?

She hung up the phone and clapped her hands together. "Well, see how crazy this business is? How's that for timing?"

17

"When do we start to work?" I asked, my voice squeaky. I knew my mom wouldn't let me cut school.

Ms. Ida looked up sharply. "Good question," she said. "Of course, you'll need a portfolio with good photographs in it. All models have to have that."

"But I thought you said we had the job," Lida said.

"Oh, you do, you do," she said sweetly. "But you never go without pictures. Polaroid snapshots just won't do." She was searching in a card file for a photographer she knew. "And of course, you don't want any old job. He just said he'd see you, and I have to send you over if I become your agent. Besides the shots, which will cost you only two hundred and fifty dollars, you'll have to learn how to be a model, how to sit, how to walk, how to do your makeup. . . ."

I tuned her out there. My mom didn't want either me or Abigail putting "all that goo" on our faces.

"And how to do your hair. Image is everything in this business!"

None of us said anything. She was spellbinding.

"But of course, you do have this job, and it will pay one hundred dollars, which we can deduct from the cost of your modeling-class tuition."

Lisa caught my eye. I stole a glance at Lida, and then we all stared back at Ms. Ida, who was now mostly engulfed in a cloud of smoke.

"I see you all live on the Upper West Side, a high-rent district, and you all go to private school." She leaned in and almost whispered, as if it were a secret, "So I know the tuition will be no sweat for you."

I wanted to say that our apartment wasn't all that great, just big, and that my mom worked so we could all go to college, and to pay for Christopher's lessons. But I felt tongue-tied, like a Muppet.

She was speaking more rapidly. "With twins we'll give you a discount, because we're getting two for the price of one. So, let's see, the whole thing for each girl, including the portfolio shots, comes to one thousand dollars, minus, of course, the one hundred-dollar fee. So that's nine hundred dollars for little Ms. Muppet and eight hundred and fifty dollars for the twins, minus the one hundred dollars for each girl. And we'll throw in pictures at no cost. What do you think, Babsi?"

"Betsi. Betsi with an *i*," I said, proud that I had said something. "It sounds great to me!" I would be special by the time I reached twelve, which was my deadline.

"Great. Classes start right after school, from four to five-thirty. We do, of course, need the tuition in full before you can begin."

I nodded vigorously.

"We'll have to think it over," Lida and Lisa said together.

"Oh, it's adorable that you can talk like that," Ms. Ida cooed. "The tuition is really a small amount when you think of all the money you can make modeling for magazines and on television commercials. Call me tomorrow," she said, and then she stood up very quickly. When she stood up I could see she was very short, almost as short as me, and that she had lipstick on her teeth. As she shook hands with us all I could barely contain my excitement. I was going to be a model! All I needed was nine hundred dollars.

The reception room was still packed with wall-to-wall kids as we made our way to the door. I almost stepped on a crawling baby. Walking to the elevator, Lisa asked, "Betsi, do you really think your parents will let you have the money to do this?"

They had to. I wanted it more than anything in the world. On the other hand, feeding Chris's daily piano habit cost money. Abigail would get a scholarship to college, but she wouldn't go unless she had her teeth straightened. Maybe my parents wouldn't have the money.

But I knew just the person to ask.

Chapter

THREE

Dear Diary,

Ten more days to go until I'm twelve.
Day Two

Diary Dear,
Yesterday I found out I could be a model. But I need $900 to do it. All day long that was all I could think about. When I came home yesterday from Kiddie Shots I couldn't get up the nerve to ask my parents. Lisa and Lida's parents said they were sorry, but they couldn't give them the money. And also they thought they were too young to work. I've got to be a model by the time I'm twelve, or at least say I'm on my way to being a model.

See, Di, when I'm a model Donny will notice me. I'll know

how to sit and stand and fix my hair. My picture will be in *Seventeen* magazine.

But I'd die if I had to ask my parents for the money. They'd just say I was special anyway, even if they didn't believe it.

I have to get the money another way. But I just need the nerve to do it. There's only one other person besides you, Di, who knows about my dream. She's never said no to me yet.

Today was a rainbow-colored day that might fade out or have a pot of gold at the end of it. I have to give it a C because I only took part of my brain to school today. But it could just very well be one of those A+ days if my dreams come true.

Love and xxx's
Betsi with an *i*

To get to my grandma's I had to take the elevator down to the ground floor and then walk all the way across the lobby to another bank of elevators. We lived in 9D, and my grandma lived in 12R. I couldn't just walk up three flights and cross over because there was a courtyard separating the two sides of the building.

When I got to her door my heart was pounding so loud I wondered if she'd be able to hear the thudding. I rang three short buzzes and one long one. That was our special signal so she'd know it was me.

"Hi, Grandma," I said when the door swung open.

She grabbed my face so that my cheeks puckered and gave me a fat, juicy kiss. As I walked in I could smell something yummy baking, something chocolate. One thing about my grandma's apartment I liked was that it was always so neat and cozy. There were knitted doilies on top of the peach-colored sofa and chairs, and there was always a vase of sweet-smelling, fresh-cut flowers on the coffee table. Our apartment was just the reverse. Everything was chaotic. I could never find anything I needed.

As I watched my grandma triple-lock the door I began to feel very nervous. But I knew I had to ask. Especially since I knew she would say yes. She walked back to the sofa, where she must have been sitting, and picked up her knitting. She wore thin gold-frame granny glasses, and she had short, silvery-white hair that she had washed and set at the beauty shop every week. She was wearing a sleeveless pink overblouse with powder-blue pants.

"When the brownies are done you'll have one with a nice cold glass of milk, yes?"

Actually I felt too nervous to eat. I have to mention that my grandma wasn't knitting to pass the time. She did it for a living. She was a pro knitter. People hired her to knit things for them. Her things were photographed for magazines, and her sweaters hung in the windows of knit shops. She was famous, and Grandpa Lester used to call her a smart cookie. That was the label she sewed inside of everything she knitted: Smart Cookie.

"What's on your mind, Betsi?" she asked, squinting over her glasses, her knitting needles clacking away. "I can always tell when you have something on your mind. Is it only one thing?"

She was shrewd.

"Spit it out, Betsi, don't repress it. Grandma loves you."

"Grandma, could I borrow some money?" I said in a high, squeaky voice.

She looked me over, put down the silver-and-hot-pink sweater she was knitting, and went to the vestibule near the front door. Her beige leather bag was hanging from the hall tree.

"Of course, Betsi darling. How much do you want? Three dollars? Will five do? Maybe you need ten?"

I shook my head miserably. "Grandma, I need a little more than that."

She put her bag back on the hook and headed for the kitchen, where she kept money in pots on the top shelf. "Do you need twenty-five dollars?" she shouted from the kitchen.

"Oh, Grandma, I need nine hundred dollars as soon as possible." Although maybe it might have been better to ask for a thousand in case I needed something else. Ms. Ida said I would be making money soon, and I could pay my grandma back shortly.

My grandma came back to the living room, walking fast. She took my chin in her hands and said, "Betsi, darling, what's wrong? Do you need an operation? No, you had your tonsils out. Are you in trouble with the police? No, you're a good girl. Did you borrow one of your mother's credit cards and go shopping? No, you'd never do that."

When my grandma got excited she always asked questions and answered every single one of them. She never waited for an answer.

"Oh, no, Grandma, it's nothing like that. I just need the money so I can get a job as a model."

She sat down and picked up her knitting, counting some stitches first. "I see" was all she said. I waited.

She put down her knitting and said, "That doesn't sound like you're being a smart cookie, Betsi. If you got a job as a model, they would pay you. You wouldn't have to pay them."

"But, Grandma, you have to be taught how to do your hair, how to sit, how to stand, and they already have a job for me at *Seventeen* magazine. They're going to deduct what the magazine will pay me. That's why it's nine hundred dollars."

Grandma picked up her knitting and nodded. "*Seven-*

teen. I knitted a sweater for them once. Nice magazine.
I know how much you want to be special, Betsi darling,
but this modeling thing sounds like a Spam to me.'

I watched her fingers fly expertly with the knitting
needles and her glasses slip down her nose.

"A spam, Grandma?" I said meekly.

"Sure. Why do you have to be taught to walk and
talk and sit and stand? You've been doing all that for
almost twelve years now. Surely you have it down by
now. I'll give you the cream rinse, and you'll go do your
hair." She never could stick to one topic at a time.
"The thing is, you already have a job. You have to go
to school, do your homework, and play with your friends.
You're too young to work, and modeling is hard work.
Come, let's have a brownie. I'll put powdered sugar on
top, and it will be all melty from the stove. I can't let
you have the money for that, Betsi. I know when I
smell a Spam."

I stared at the bowl with fresh peaches on the coffee
table until I figured it out. "Spam? Grandma, isn't that
the spicy luncheon meat in a tin can?"

'That's right," she said.

Suddenly I had it. "Grandma, do you mean scam?
You think the modeling course is a scam?"

"That's what I said, Betsi, darling. It's a Spam, and
not for a smart cookie. Now how about some brownies
and milk?"

I followed my grandma into the kitchen, with its clock

made in the shape of a big, round apple, and sat down at the small table with its yellow and white checkered tablecloth. The yummy smell of warm, rich chocolate took my mind off my troubles for a second or two. I was eleven days away from being twelve, and I still wasn't anyone special. The only good thing was I could have two brownies. No one would care if I got a zit or gained a pound.

"Grandma, you make the best brownies in the whole world," I said with my mouth full.

"Eat, eat."

"It wasn't that I was dying to be a model so much, Grandma," I said between bites. "It's just that Abbie gets all As, and Chris is preparing for another concert, and I'm going to be twelve, and I don't do anything special. I'm a misfit in my own family."

She poured me another glass of milk and handed me my second brownie. "Well, I think you're special, Betsi, darling. You don't have to do anything to be it. Give yourself time. There might be something you're special at but haven't developed yet." She passed me a third brownie and refilled my glass with bubbling cold milk. "But I definitely think you're special, Betsi. You have a certain something."

"A certain what?" I almost pleaded.

"A certain something. Don't ask me to explain it in words. You'll find out. But you have it. I always knew you did."

She kissed me on my nose, and that's when I had my brilliant brainstorm.

"Grandma, how do you make these brownies?"

"This is a very old recipe. It came from my mother, your great-grandmother, who got it from her mother, who got it from her aunt Ida. May she rest in peace." We paused with respect. We did that a lot when anyone mentioned my grandpa Lester, who died when I was nine years old. He and my grandma owned a knitting shop.

"Grandma, I want to sell your brownies," I said, suddenly seeing myself as a business person. I trailed her back to the living room.

"Sell my brownies? Why, Betsi, whatever for? I'll gladly give them away. I can't eat the whole batch myself."

'Oh, no, no,' I said, shaking my head and feeling my curls bounce. "I mean let's go into business. You'll make them, and I'll sell them. And then I'll be a twelve-year-old kid business whiz, and I could be written up in *New York* magazine, and we could have it laminated for my room."

She smiled over the tops of her thin-rimmed glasses, put her knitting in her lap, and leaned back on the sofa. She said simply, "Oh, I see."

"But, Grandma, can we change the recipe a bit? Make it different? Because there are a lot of brownies on the market. They're all chocolate, they all have nuts. Sometimes there's even vanilla ice cream inside."

Grandma thought a moment. "Something different. I understand." She took up her knitting again, miraculously never dropping a stitch in her intricate pattern.

"Something different, special. I understand," she said again.

"Like a wild ingredient that will give it a little kick," I said.

My grandma leaned toward me. "What kind of a little kick?"

There was a framed needlepoint picture on the wall I saw all the time but had never really looked at. It had three big, juicy strawberries in the center of it.

"That's it!" I shouted, pointing to the needlepoint hanging. "I've got it!"

"Needlepoint brownies? Oh, I don't think anyone would want to eat those."

"No. We'll be the first business people to make strawberry brownies. They'll be a luscious, dreamy, strawberry shade and taste like strawberries instead of brownie brownies!"

"That's it!" my grandma shouted. Then she got very quiet. "But, Betsi, how do we do that?"

"We'll invent it!" I said, still excited.

"Well, we *could* take the chocolate brownie recipe I use and then just substitute strawberries for chocolate, I guess. Then again, I have some strawberry preserves."

She was knitting faster and faster, almost at breakneck speed. "I have some frozen strawberries also, and some red food coloring. It might work, and it certainly is original."

She and I jumped up and hugged each other. Then we dashed into the kitchen and plunged right in. The first thing I did was to get a pad of paper so I could begin to take orders for the world's first strawberry brownies. Meanwhile, my grandma took out her bowls and got all the ingredients together.

Tammy, who was my best friend, would love these. Strawberry was her first favorite flavor. Tammy was the current president of our club, the Double A's, named after our bra sizes.

I called her while Grandma was mixing the pink batter and explained to her that I was going into the catering business and baking brownies. Strawberry brownies.

"Why?" she asked. "Did your dad get fired?"

Tammy ended up, after my super sales pitch, ordering two dozen because I told her everyone would take that many, and also I reminded her of her strawberry habit. I could hear my grandma singing one of her old Russian folk melodies while she was working. I went in and dipped my finger into the peppermint-pink batter that she was working on. It already tasted like a cross between pink cotton candy and crunchy strawberry cookies.

"Oh, Grandma. They're going to be fantastic! What

should we name them? Grandma's Pinkies would be a nice name.''

She put her hands up, laughing. "Wait, we'll see after we mix them all and bake them. But, Betsi, they should be named after you. This is your discovery.'' Secretly I was glad. Who wants to go on Johnny Carson as a twelve-year-old whiz kid with a name like My Grandma's Brownies? But what could we call them? We needed something very catchy, a way-out, wildly exotic, totally unforgettable name.

Chapter

FOUR

"I got it!" I shouted. "What about Betsi's Strawberry Brownies?"

'That has a ring to it. Yes, I like it," my grandma said. "But, Betsi, darling, it's six-thirty. You should call your mother and ask her if you can stay for dinner. Then we can finish mixing another batch and bake them all."

I looked at the apple clock on her wall and called downstairs. Then I told my grandma, "Mom said I can stay as long as I'm not imposing."

There wasn't time for a hot dinner with lamb chops and mashed potatoes and peas and carrots and stuff like that. But my grandma always had a lot of interesting things in her refrigerator. I pulled out chopped liver, deluxe tuna salad, Bermuda onions, Swiss cheese, dill pickles, and some black bread and began to make the kind of sandwich you can't even fit your mouth around.

My grandma didn't seem to be hungry. She was singing, "Li, la, lee."

I knew I had to be very businesslike to be a kid biz whiz. How much should I charge per brownie? For starters, I figured out just one dollar. It was even change. But when we sold to better stores I would charge a dollar and a quarter. So Tammy owed me twenty-four dollars for the brownies she ordered. Maybe I would give her a fifty-cent discount for being my very best friend.

Actually we had been best friends before Morgan and before the Double A's. For a while we even looked a little alike, or at least people said we did. But then Tammy grew taller and thinner than me. She was willowy looking now. Maybe because she took ballet lessons every day after school. Her hair was curly like mine but was softer and medium brown, and she pushed it up and back and fastened it with a clip. Her eyes reminded me of large root-beer Life Savers. I decided she was prettier than me.

I finished my sandwich and decided to call the next girl on my list, my Double A club sister, Kelly. Kelly's mom and dad, Mr. and Mrs. Gonzales, were divorced, and her mom worked as a legal secretary and was dating a man Kelly didn't like. At least not as much as she liked her real father, who didn't know Kelly's mom was dating someone.

I wished I had hair like Kelly's. She wore it short, and it was sleek and glossy black. It kind of hugged her head like a helmet. She was the only one of us who didn't have any brothers or sisters, so I had to tease her a lot. Sometimes, though, I wished I were in her shoes.

"Kelly?" I asked after I reached her. "Listen, everyone's in on this." I knew Kelly had a fear of being left out. She would order brownies if everyone did.

"What? What is it?"

"Well, I've decided to go into business for myself. I've invented a new brownie."

"What was wrong with the old one?"

I glanced at my grandma. Her face was strawberry red, her hair was falling in her eyes, and she looked like she was having a good time working on another batch of brownies. "My brownies," I explained to Kelly, who was the practical one of us, "are different. My brownies are pink, and they taste like strawberries." At least I hoped they would taste like strawberries.

"Betsi, that doesn't make sense. Everyone knows brownies are chocolate. Why would anyone buy strawberry brownies? People count on brownies being chocolate. I love brownies. I like them the way they are. It doesn't make sense to make strawberry brownies."

I sighed to myself. Kelly had no imagination. She was always so scientific. She would probably become a nuclear physicist or something. Then I thought of the science project I was supposed to be working on right then but immediately pushed it out of my mind. I was good at pushing things out of my mind, and besides, inventing strawberry brownies was scientific, wasn't it?

"Okay, I'll take one," she said reluctantly.

"One? Kelly, you can't eat just one." Besides, that would only be a dollar. But I didn't tell her that.

I finally persuaded her to take two. Then I marked down on my pad that I had made twenty-five dollars and fifty cents. My grandma was singing even louder now, bustling about the kitchen.

"La, li, lee," sang my grandma as she danced around the kitchen. When all cake pans containing Betsi's Strawberry Brownies finally went into the oven it was eight o'clock. I helped her clean up, and then we went into the living room to wait.

My grandma's knitting needles began to clack faster. I started to bite my fingernails. When the timer on the stove went off we almost bumped into each other hurrying into the kitchen to see what we had. Cautiously, we opened the oven. There were six pans of glowing pink brownies. We pulled them out one by one. It took just a second to get used to the idea that we weren't smelling the intoxicating aroma of warm, rich chocolate but of strawberries. We waited for them to cool before my grandma cut out perfect rectangle bars in a dreamy, scrumptious shade of pink. They were unbelievable.

"You first," I said to her. "You baked them."

"Oh, no," she protested. "It was all your idea."

I closed my eyes and bit off a corner of one, concentrating as I munched away. Then I opened my eyes wide. "Grandma, we did it!" She took one, closed her eyes, bit into it, and opened her eyes so wide I thought her glasses would slip totally off her nose.

"Not too tart, not too sweet," she said, chewing.

"Unbelievably delicious!" I added.

Really. Picture biting into a pink brownie that was entirely strawberry tasting but had the consistency of a brownie brownie. Strawberry brownies!

"Maybe a teeny bit more chopped-up strawberry," Grandma said as I grabbed her waist and waltzed her around the kitchen. Pretty soon I would be taller than she was.

"Oh, Grandma, I love you!" I shouted.

"I can't remember when I've had more fun," she said.

It was a little before nine when we packed everything up. I still had some homework to do and had to put some last-minute touches on my science project: "Bugs Indigenous to North America." It was a yucky assignment. That was why I put it off. But then I put everything off to the last minute when it came to homework. My sister had been working on her science project for the last three months. Hers would be better, obviously. But I had strawberry brownies, and I would be the first twelve-year-old kid at my school to be in business for herself.

My grandma gave me my batches of strawberry brownies in plastic supermarket bags. Then the two orders went in paper bags. Someday I would have pink bags with Betsi with an *i* on them. She threw in a few of the old-fashioned, now obsolete, chocolate brownies. I kissed her good night and went down in the elevator to cross the lobby and go back up on the other elevator to my apartment.

No one saw me creep in with my bags, but I heard everyone. Chris was playing the piano. I heard a television. There was the clacking of mom's typewriter. She really worked hard, I decided. I tiptoed into the kitchen and carefully put the paper bags with Kelly's and Tammy's orders on the kitchen counter. I hadn't called Lisa and Lida, but they were pushovers. When they saw these they would buy them on the spot. Then I took out a good china plate and arranged the pink squares so everyone in my family could taste one. Boy, were they going to be surprised. Then, as an afterthought, I put some of Grandma's brownie brownies on another plate. She'd probably never bake them again. Then I covered everything with Saran Wrap so the brownies would stay fresh.

Exhausted, I went back to my all-powder-blue room. Everything was powder blue—the bedspread, my desk, the curtains, the wallpaper, the rug, a coffee mug, etc. It was like living inside a birthday cake.

My science project was propped up against the wall,

and I saw three bugs had slipped out from under the pushpins and were now on the floor. The pushpins were in every color, but the bugs were mostly the same, just different sizes with hard-to-pronounce names. I scrambled to put the bugs back. It had taken me a long time to find them. I didn't intend to lose any.

Abigail's project was much more elaborate, to say the least. Hers was about interplanetary travel in the year 2050. The planets were made of Christmas ornaments and large balls, and the smaller moons and things were marbles. It had batteries and lights so it lit up in sections. She had strung wires to indicate the space travel routes, and she had used three rolls of tinfoil for the background. It was really super, and her science teacher was already thinking about entering it in the New York State science fair.

As I climbed into bed and snuggled under the covers I knew I was finally on my way with Betsi's Strawberry Brownies. I always knew I had a flair for business. Of course, it would probably take a little work to get into the larger stores, and I'd have to have a lot of publicity. But what the heck, when you've got a dynamite product, you've got everything. Tired but happier than I'd been in a long time, I reached over and set my powder-blue alarm clock for seven-thirty so I'd have time to write in my diary before school.

Dear Diary,

Nine days to go until I'm twelve.
Day Three.

Good morning, Diary. Well, I did it. I guess I won't be a model like I thought, but I will be a business kid, a kind of entrepreneur. My name will go down in history. Every kid who gets pimples from eating chocolate will love me. Maybe I should dot the *i* on Betsi with a tiny little strawberry.

Anyway, by the time I'm twelve I will have made it.

I wonder what Donny will say. Maybe I'll get up the nerve to sell him some. As far as I know, he doesn't like anyone special. Maybe it could be me.

Today when I go to school everyone will be different because I'm different now. Di, I will be special by the time I'm twelve, probably before.

Love and xxx's
Betsi with an *i*

I tucked my diary back in my drawer and dragged my big board of North American bugs out of my room and into the hall. Then I went into the kitchen for my strawberry brownies, my beautiful pink brownies.

But they weren't there. The chocolate brownies were all gone, too, except for some little bits of crumbs.

I couldn't figure it out. Had my family eaten all my strawberry brownies? The only things on the strawberry brownie plate were little buglike things.

My bug collection was still in the hall, I knew.

Someone had played a trick on me.

They had substituted my perfectly rectangular, absolutely exquisite pink brownies for these weird little shriveled-up pink balls. What were they, exactly?

I had only a few minutes to get out the door!

As I was running out I spotted three notes on the table. All of them were written on the same piece of yellow lined paper.

The first note said:

Betsi,

Tell Grandma to stick to her chocolate brownies. These new ones just don't shape up. And tell Grandma to come over soon. Tell her we love her, and if it wouldn't be an imposition, could she bring some of her brownies? What about Saturday night for dinner? Have a nice day and don't forget your bugs.

Dad

What happened to my strawberry brownies?

The next note was from Abbie and was the last straw, or so I thought:

What are those vile little pink thingies?
Are they part of your bug collection? Can I use them for
my science project as little space ships? You know pink is
my color.

What happened to my strawberry brownies?
The last note from Chris really got to me:

Betsi, what are those things? I ate one.
Will I die?

They were gone. My strawberry brownies were gone,
and I didn't know how or why. In their place were
pieces of bubble gum or erasers. I started to cry. I
reached for the phone to cry with my grandma, but it
was too early to call her. It was also going to be too late
to take the bus to school.

Then I remembered! Kelly and Tammy's bags of
brownies. If someone was playing a joke on me, no one
would have found those bags. So the real Betsi's Strawberry Brownies were still around. I ripped open the
bags to find the magical strawberry brownies that were
to be my claim to fame and fortune. Horrified, I picked
out one of those shriveled-up little puckery pink thingies.

Tears rolled down my cheeks as I realized those were
Betsi's Strawberry Brownies. I wondered what we did
wrong. Was it a little something we left out? An ingredient we put in that we shouldn't have? I didn't have time
to think about it then.

Now I really was going to be late for school. I would have to go to school in a cab. To do that I would have to lose two more minutes turning my piggy bank upside down for the money. It didn't cost too much to get to Morgan. I dumped out about four dollars in quarters, dimes, and nickels. Then I slid my big board into the hall with the handles of the bags of pink buggies in my mouth. Downstairs the doorman, Jimmy, carried my board and hailed me a cab. It's hard to be my age and hail a cab, especially with a board full of bugs. Cab drivers think you're fooling around, and they won't stop.

When I told the driver where I was going he said, "Nice. When I was your age I used to take the bus to school—not a cab."

"My business flopped," I said in a low voice. Was it the food coloring? Were the strawberries bad? Was the oven too hot? Did my grandma put something in that shouldn't have been there? I brushed a tear off my face and looked out the window as the taxi meter went up. What had happened to Betsi's Strawberry Brownies?

"Oh, I am sorry," the cabbie said sarcastically. "Listen, things are bad all over."

When I got out in front of Morgan I paid the cab driver carefully in quarters, nickels, and dimes. He told me to consider taking vitamins. Then I dragged my big board up the walk to the gates and gingerly slid it up the two steps to the main door. Panicked, I realized three bugs were missing, so I had to prop the board against the stairs and retrace my steps looking for the bugs I'd dropped. At least it wasn't raining, I told myself.

I was late, but there were still a few stragglers in the hall. One of them said, "Hey, Betsi, one of your bugs dropped. Whoops, you just stepped on it."

I stooped down to get it and tried to puff it up before pinning it back on.

All I could think of was that at lunchtime I would run out and find a pay phone and call my grandma. She'd have the answer. Everything would be all right again, and I would still be the kid genius behind Betsi's Strawberry Brownies.

What had happened that morning was just a slight miscalculation.

My grandma would know what to do.

I just had to hang in until I could talk to her.

Chapter

FIVE

I saw Tammy before she saw me. She was wearing a yellow turtleneck and jeans. She must have just washed her fluffy hair, because it was sticking straight up and formed a halo around her head.

"Betsi! Betsi! Wait up! It's time for lunch!"

She ran after me, and her feet turned out like a duck's, as if she had the wrong ankles on the wrong legs. That was from taking ballet lessons for so long.

"I'll see you later!" I shouted. I had only a little time. Across the street from school was a tiny candy store with a pay phone wedged in between the magazines and a dusty gumball machine. I had a quarter in my pocket and was trembling. I dialed my grandma's number and hoped she would be in.

I was in tears when she finally answered the phone.

"Oh, Grandma, the strawberry brownies shrank overnight into these crumbly little buggy thingies. Oh, Grandma, what could have gone wrong?"

"Oh, Betsi, not Betsi's Strawberry Brownies? Now tell me exactly what happened," Grandma said.

"I don't know what happened. I thought you might," I cried. "Grandma, can you make another batch so we can find out how to fix them?"

There was an awesome silence on the other end of the phone.

"Oh, Betsi, darling. I don't know how to break the news to you. But the recipes I combined together to make the brownies—well, I was in such a good mood, singing and dancing. I can't remember when I've had so much fun, and—"

I began to feel slightly sick to my stomach. "And what, Grandma?"

"Well, I threw away the recipes by mistake, Betsi, dear."

I was getting panicked that my time would run out. "Quick, Grandma, where did you throw them? We can rescue them!"

There was another awesome silence.

"I put them in the incinerator, Betsi, dear."

"Oh, Grandma, they were so yummy, and then they got so yucky. Can you maybe guess what might have gone wrong? And how we could redo them?"

She was thinking. I was afraid any minute the operator would cut in and ask for more money. I didn't have any more change.

"Vanilla, Betsi. Maybe we should have added vanilla, but then again, I don't see how vanilla could have affected them. Maybe, well—I just don't know. But, Betsi, I promise you I'll work on them."

My life had been ruined. There were no more Betsi's Brownies. By the time I was twelve I wouldn't be a model and I wouldn't be a kid biz whiz. There were only nine days left, and I had to think of something—fast!

Quickly I blurted out, "Grandma, Daddy says he loves your brownies and to come over for dinner Saturday night and bring a couple dozen with you."

"He loves my brownies?"

The operator cut in, and then I heard my grandma asking me for the number of the pay phone, but it was too late. I was staring at a dead phone.

"Are you done?" a man behind me said.

I had no more change, so I turned and raced back across the street to school. I wasn't hungry at all. I found only a package of stale peanuts in my locker, so I decided not to eat anything. I slammed my locker door angrily. I turned around and found myself eyeball to eyeball with the twins, Lisa and Lida. I wondered how long they'd been watching me.

"Look, Betsi," Lisa said, hands on her hips, "we're calling an emergency meeting of the Double A's tomorrow morning at Tammy's house."

"What's the meeting about?" I asked, dropping my books. "What's the emergency?"

"You," Lisa said.

"Yeah," Lida said. "You've been acting a little strange lately, and we're worried about you, Betsi."

They walked away without another word, their long, light-blond hair swishing back and forth, their tight jeans hugging them in all the right places, the red on their sweaters exactly matching the red of their bulky socks. Boy, if I could have been a twin, I would never have to worry about being special. But then my twin might have been a boy, and that would have been totally gross.

My last class of the day was science with Mr. Biderman, and I couldn't help noticing how loud my stomach was rumbling. I waited breathlessly when he got to my big board, praying I hadn't lost any more bugs. He stroked his red mustache and said, "Well, Betsi did a bug collection, following in the tradition of her leaf collection in the fall." That's all he said. Cheryl got a B+ for "Molecules in Motion." It was nice. Terry got an A for his map of ancient Egypt using multicolored sand. I got a C and thought if I hadn't lost as many bugs as I had maybe I would have gotten a C+.

As I came out of class Tammy was right behind me. She got a B on her studies of feet. She stopped at her locker for her dance bag that was shaped like a watermelon slice. I opened my locker, which had a picture of

Godzilla taped to it, and took out some books I knew I would be too depressed to look at.

"Hey, Betsi," Tammy said suddenly, "where are your strawberry brownies?"

"Oh, well, they didn't turn out. Save your money," I said, feeling even worse.

"I didn't bring it anyway. My mother wouldn't let me have that much unless it was for a good cause. You look really sad. How about riding the bus with me to my ballet class?"

We linked arms, and I said, "It must be great to take ballet lessons. You must feel special. It makes you stand out."

Tammy laughed. "My mother makes me take them."

About fifteen minutes later, after taking the crosstown bus, we were standing on Broadway and Eighty-sixth Street in front of Tammy's ballet studio, Miss Violet's. I could hear the piano music drifting down to the street.

"Well, I guess I'll see you at the meeting tomorrow," she said, and then she walked away with her feet turned out.

I ran up Broadway, trying to figure something I could do or be—in a hurry.

I tried for a couple of steps to run like a ballet dancer, with my feet turned out like a duck's. But I tripped. It sure must be hard to be a ballerina.

At the door the doorman handed me a note from my grandma. Who else? This time it was written on hot pink paper with white polka dots and said:

Betsi, darling,
   Think of it this way. Being in business for yourself isn't so hot. You never get time off, nobody gives you a paycheck, you never get a vacation. What's wrong, Betsi dear, with just being Betsi?

Grandma loves you

P.S. Tell your daddy I'll be there Saturday night with as many brownies as I can make. And I'm sorry, Betsi, darling, they won't be the pink kind.

I stuffed my grandma's wonderful note into my navy blazer. Then I went down the hall and waited for the elevator. I was so much closer to my grandma than Abbie and Chris were, but then again, they were always too busy to see her much.

After I let myself into our apartment I started straight for my room to get away from Chris's practicing and Abbie's bragging about the grade she had gotten on her science project.

But before I could turn my doorknob to fade into my powder-blue room in powder-blue misery my mom tapped me on the shoulder. She was wearing a T-shirt that said "Munsen's Marmalade." Her Mets baseball cap was turned to the side, and I knew she was writing advertising copy.

"Betsi," she said, "I hate to bother you, because I know you want to do your homework." Groan. I hadn't thought of that.

"That's okay, Mom," I said.

"Well, I'm thinking up names for china patterns." She showed me some pictures of plates with different designs. "This is the one I need a name for."

I looked at it. It was a white plate, like all the rest of them, but this one had swirls of green leaves and gold around the rim.

"I need a name that's regal! Rich! Tasteful! The kind of china you would use for very special company. I'm sick of naming plates, and I'm stuck on this one, Betsi. I need the name by tomorrow."

"Uh-huh."

"See, the plates have this dark green leafy pattern, but then there's also this swirl of rich gold."

"Uh-huh," I said. I sure felt depressed. I didn't know if I could help her out.

"And I know what a flair you have for thinking up things that are clever, Betsi, dear. Am I imposing? Should I ask you later?"

"I'd call it Evergreen," I said.

My mom looked at the plate, looked at me, twisted her hat, and then gave me a tight squeeze and a hug and ran off to her little office in the back. I guessed it was okay. Before she had children she had worked at a big advertising agency we had nicknamed Mudd,

Fudd, Creep, and Crud. Of course, that wasn't its real name.

Softly I shut the door to my room and went to the drawer where I kept my diary. I felt so miserable I just had to write in it one more time that day. Life is full of surprises, that's for sure. I had expected to write that we were besieged with orders for Betsi's Strawberry Brownies, that we had hired people to bake them, and that I'd booked myself onto a local talk show. But the truth was a whole lot different.

Dear Diary,

Still nine days until twelve.
Still Day Three.

Diary, dear, I don't know how to tell you this, but Betsi's Strawberry Brownies turned into strawberry bugs. Grandma doesn't know what happened. Only a scientist could know for sure. It's too late to start over, and besides, I couldn't take the disappointment again if they didn't work.

My life is over, Di, and I have no ideas. If I could just think of something. I have to be special by the time I'm twelve because I made this deadline for myself, and because I spent all my time being eleven as an invisible person.

So I have nine and a half more days, and Di, time flies. I just have to come up with something. Do you have any ideas?

What can I say about today? It was a buggy day, kind of a watercolor wash between slate gray and nauseating dull brown. No grade for today. It was so awful I would just have to give it an incomplete.

Love and xxx's
Betsi with an *i*

As I put away my beautiful powder-blue satin diary I was aware of quiet little sobs coming from the living room. I ran into the living room not knowing what to think. I never know what to think in my house. There was Lutzy, Chris's flamboyant piano teacher, shredding the scarf he always wore. It was black with white piano keys on it. Maybe Chris had made a clunker of a mistake, and Lutzy was having a nervous breakdown.

My mom was sitting on the couch quietly crying. Abbie had come home from school, and even she was looking sad. The doorbell rang, and surprise of surprises, in came my grandma, and she was crying.

Oh, no, I thought. Something had happened to my dad. Maybe one of his patients had done something violent to him. Being a psychologist was hard. Patients felt all kinds of weird things about their doctor.

And then I saw Chris.

He was hiding under the piano. On his right hand was a huge white cast. It looked like a boxing glove.

"Dummkopf!" Lutzy screamed. "How could you break

your hand when we have a concert scheduled, the most important concert of your career?''

Chris stuttered through his tears. ''But Lutzy, all I did was play a little baseball with the guys.''

Chris wasn't very good at sports. He was always too busy playing the piano to practice any games.

Lutzy put his hands on his head and shook it back and forth. ''The programs, the hall, the reviewers, the after-concert reception. He'll never be ready now. We'll have to change the date.'' Then Lutzy screamed in frustration. ''Dummkopf! You're an artist. You can't take chances.''

He put on his jacket, fluffed out what was left of his piano scarf, plunked on a beret, and kissed my mother's hand. He swept out the door, not even looking at poor Chris, who was still hiding under the Steinway.

Even when Chris was temporarily un-special he was special. I wondered what would happen.

Chapter
SIX

I had about ten minutes that Saturday morning to get to the emergency meeting at Tammy's. She lived on Ninety-sixth Street and Central Park West, so I ran there. I kept trying to figure out what it was they wanted to talk to me about.

Tammy's apartment faced Central Park. Sometimes we could see horseback riders winding through the bridle paths, dodging branches. One night I slept over, and when we woke up it had snowed. All the surfaces were white and icy and connected by snow. It looked as if the trees were holding hands.

I loved Tammy's room. It had a bed with a white ruffly canopy, a pink fluffy rug, and a white desk with red drawers, and all along the walls were pictures of girls in ballet costumes.

When we were all there Kelly said shyly, "Gee, I love your room," as if Tammy had just gotten it. We were sitting cross-legged on her pink shag rug. Pink. Suddenly I hated the color. Ugh. Why did my beautiful pink strawberry brownies have to shrink and shrivel?

Tammy shrugged. "This stuff comes and goes." Her dad was an actor in a top soap opera. He played Biff on "All My Sorrows" now, but before this show he had been a struggling actor and had had to sell property in Florida, sight unseen, work as a singing waiter, and act off-Broadway, which paid very little. Tammy's mom had worked as a legal secretary then. Now she designed and sold silver jewelry.

I started biting my nails long before the meeting started.

"Okay," Tammy said. "This meeting has been called about *you*." Everyone stared at me.

"Why?" I asked, immediately on the defensive.

There was an awkward silence. Then Lisa and Lida spoke at once. "The modeling."

"What was wrong with the modeling? You went," I said.

"Yeah," Lida said. "But we went along for the fun of it. You treated it like a life-and-death matter."

"Let's face it, you haven't been yourself, Betsi," Tammy said. "You've been acting like something's really bothering you. As your club sisters, we have a right to know what it is."

"That's right," Lisa and Lida said in unison.

Everyone waited for me to say something. But my problem was a secret between me and my diary. I braided the hairs of the shag rug nervously.

"Out with it, Bets," Tammy said. "Remember who you are? You're a Double A. That's what we're here for."

"Oh, well, the thing is . . ." I mumbled inaudibly.

"Could you speak up?" Kelly prompted.

"Well, the thing is I'll be twelve in about eight days, and I'm just not anything special. I don't do anything." I looked around the room. Kelly was good at sports. Tammy was a ballerina. Lisa and Lida were beautiful twins. I mean, they could have been ugly twins. "I don't do anything. I'm not something."

"Are you saying that because your sister has an unbroken record of straight As, and because a reporter did a newspaper article on her?" Tammy asked.

I nodded miserably.

"Are you saying this just because your little brother, Christopher, is already a concert pianist at the age of nine?" Kelly continued.

I nodded again, and this time my eyes were brimming with tears. Okay, so my secret was out. I was this un-special middle child, and it was driving me crazy. I could feel my face turning red because it was humiliating for everyone to know how I felt.

"Well, I happen to think your brother's a little nerdy," Lisa said.

"Me, too," Lida said.

"Oh, guess what? He broke his hand. I think his concert's off," I said.

Tammy reached for a jar of unsalted peanuts on her desk and passed them around. "Oh, it will heal. They'll probably take him to a specialist, and it'll get better twice as fast," Tammy said, stretching out on the rug.

"You know, Abbie's not that pretty," Lisa said, sitting back to back with Lida. They did that a lot, stretched out like bookends. "I don't think she has a lot of friends," Lida said. "Abbie has an attitude."

"If you're trying to prove they aren't special, forget it," Kelly said crisply. "We can't make Betsi an accomplished musician or even manage to put one A on her report card. So your deadline is eight days, Betsi?"

"Yeah. Next Sunday is my twelfth birthday."

Tammy dumped a handful of peanuts in my palm.

"But you're popular in school. Everyone says that. You're very outgoing. Everyone likes you. Chris and Abbie aren't very popular. Maybe it's because they're so wrapped up in themselves," Tammy said. "They don't have what it takes. And you do!"

I really wasn't paying attention. "I wanted to be a model," I said sadly.

"I would forget about that," Lisa and Lida said together.

"Then I wanted to be a business wizard with my strawberry brownies."

"I'd forget about that," everyone said together.

Then we turned and saw Tammy pounding the rug. "Wait, I've got it! I've got it!" She stood up. "Listen," she said, screaming. "You need a boyfriend to be special. And you can do it before you're twelve!"

I screamed. Lisa and Lida toppled over and rolled around on the floor. Kelly, who hardly ever smiled, was laughing so hard tears were dripping down her cheeks.

"Oh, my goodness," I said. "Do you know what you just said? If I had a boyfriend, I would be the only sixth-grade girl going—going—"

"Going steady," Lisa supplied.

"With a real boy," I said. "This would require a miracle. No one has ever done it!"

"Then you'd be special." Tammy got pencils and sheets of paper. She was dead serious. Tammy believed the way to get anything done was to make a list. And then make lists on your lists.

"But who or whom would I be—am I going to be—going steady with? *Who's the boy?*"

"Well," Tammy said, "we'll make lists of all the boys Betsi can go steady with. Then we'll narrow our lists and vote. That'll be the boy."

"Just like that?" Kelly said, pacing the room. "I don't think we should do this. It's just not right."

"What's not right about it?" Tammy asked. "No one's going to come up to Betsi and say, 'Well, gee, Betsi, I'm dying to go steady with you, and especially in the next eight days,' huh?"

"Well," Kelly said, sitting cross-legged again, "you see, that's not the way it's done in the movies or on television. Two people fall in love, and usually the man goes after the woman. No one picks a name from a list of likely candidates and votes on him!" Then I remembered Kelly felt funny about these things. She had once told me she wasn't going to have a boyfriend until college.

Tammy gave us each a piece of paper. "You have to think positively," she said enthusiastically. "We are going to make Betsi the most talked-about girl in the sixth grade. I personally think a lot of boys want to go steady. No one has really let them know it's okay. Also, I think they are really shy. Betsi will be special by the time she's twelve, and she won't have to be a model or bake brownies!"

Everyone applauded, and finally Kelly did, too. Then we rolled all over the rug, laughing and punching one another.

Tammy took charge again. "Okay, everyone, number from one to five. Start with the best choice as number

59

one. Then we'll compare lists and see who Betsi's new steady boyfriend will be.''

Suddenly I saw what Kelly meant. Tammy was doing this as if we were writing a grocery list. I sucked on the end of my ballpoint pen. It might work, of course. It all depended on the boy we picked. I already knew the boy I wanted.

Tammy tuned in some soft, romantic mood music on her radio. I stole a look at Lida's list, and she saw me and shot me a dirty look, covering up her list with her elbow. After only ten minutes Tammy turned down the radio and inquired, "Okay, Double A's, what do we have?"

Lisa read her list first. "Okay, here goes:

1. Gary
2. Barry
3. Todd
4. David
5. Donny."

"Donny Delbert?" Kelly asked, a question in her voice.

"There's only one Donny," Lisa said, and I thought she sounded a little angry.

Then Kelly said, "I want you all to know that I philosophically do not believe in what we are doing."

"Read your list," we all said together.

"Okay, here's the list I don't believe in:

1. Barry
2. Gary
3. David
4. Jeffrey
5. Donny."

Lida and Tammy read their lists, and I thought it was nothing short of amazing that Donny was number five on everyone's list. I thought Donny was the cutest, nicest, smartest, coolest, most popular boy in the sixth grade. Strange. Everyone had put him last. Except for me. I read my list next.

1. Donny
2. Jeffrey
3. Sean
4. Barry
5. Gary

There was a pause. "Well, I think Gary is a lot cuter, but Barry gets good grades, and he's really nice. But Gary *is* cuter than Barry. I don't know. Who do you think Betsi should go steady with?" Tammy asked.

Something fishy was going on.

Nobody paid any attention to me. Now they were picking between Gary and Barry, with Sean as third runner-up.

"Wait a second," I yelled, and then I put two fingers

inside my mouth and whistled through my teeth. That shut everybody up.

"How come you all have Donny as number five, and I have him as number one?"

"Well, he's not right for this," Lisa said quickly.

"No, he's not the boy," said Lida.

"But I like him!" I said loudly.

I looked at each of my club sisters, and they looked everywhere but at me. Then I knew! It was as clear as mud. They put Donny as the last choice because every single Double A had a crush on Donny, too!

Tammy saw I knew. Finally she threw up her hands and said, "Okay, okay, it should be Donny if you like him." I thought that was the point.

"But you have to promise to go steady with him only for the rest of the sixth grade so that in the seventh grade one of us gets a chance," Kelly said. Boy, talk about changing your mind. Seventh grade was a little bit away from college.

I felt an anxiety attack begin. It all sounded so easy. We had picked the boy I wanted to pick, but he wasn't any old boy. How could I tell the Double A's what only my diary knew? I couldn't even talk to Donny.

I ran home even faster than I had run to Tammy's. My whole life had changed. I forgot to say hi to the doorman. I slammed the door to my room when I got in and yanked out my diary.

Dear Diary,

Eight days to go until twelve.
Day Four.

Just when I thought everything was wrong—it's right. My Double A club sisters came to my rescue. I will be special by twelve because I'll have a boyfriend, the only boyfriend in the sixth grade. And guess who, Di? Donny! There isn't anything the Double A's can't do. Well, aren't we the greatest girls' club in Morgan? The Double A's will take care of everything. Soon I'll be speaking in sentences instead of feeling like I have organic peanut butter in my mouth when I'm around him.

I'll be going steady with him. Think what everyone in school, not to mention what my family, will say about this.

Really, Diary dear, just when I thought my life was ruined, it will begin at twelve. Of course, we'll have eight more heavy days to go. Nothing more can happen on Day Four, because it's only Saturday night. I'm just so excited. Today? Oh, definitely an A+, and gold spangled over powder-blue and hot-pink satin—all under a sunshiny sky. Let's face it, DD, today was a winner. An A+.

Love and xxx's
Betsi with an *i*

When I strolled into the kitchen I was surprised to

find my grandma cooking dinner. I had thought she was invited to dinner. "Your mother had an emergency. She had to meet with an art director to plan an ad campaign for dog food. It has to be ready by Monday. Now, isn't it nice to have a mother that's such a smart cookie, Betsi?"

I knew my mom was every bit of that, and I was proud of her. I also knew that my dad couldn't help. He didn't know how to do anything but put the dishes in the dishwasher. Abbie was really busy and had been since early morning, sewing this thing for her home ec class. I think it was supposed to be an apron.

"Betsi, darling, it's so good to see you and so nice to be invited to dinner. Be a good girl and hand me the paprika."

"Grandma," I blurted out—because in the end there wasn't much I could keep from her—"I'm going to have a boyfriend."

"Well, those are always nice to have," she said. "Now find me the fat noodles." Nobody makes Hungarian goulash like my grandma. "Who are you going to have?" she said. "Tell me about him."

I stood in the middle of the kitchen floor and said proudly, "Donny Delbert. The cutest, most popular, smartest, nicest boy in all of sixth grade, both classes combined."

"And how did he ask you?" She was chopping onions and crying.

"Well, that's the thing, Grandma. He didn't ask me. The way we do it is—well, I ask him."

My grandma was just about to say something when my mom rushed into the kitchen, kissed Grandma, and poured herself a cup of coffee. "You're a lifesaver, Mother Paulson," she said.

Then Abigail ran in and grabbed a celery stalk from the refrigerator, kissing Grandma and dropping her shiny silver thimble onto the floor.

At that moment Chris came in and showed us his big white cast, thrusting it in my face. "Look!" he said. There was an autograph on his cast done in purple Magic Marker. It said "Grandma loves you."

Then my dad stepped into the kitchen and kissed Grandma, and the whole family had filled the kitchen. But then my mom had to run off to type her dog food copy. Dad wandered out with her. Abigail sighed and went back to her sewing. Chris hung around for a little while, but he never stayed in one place too long. Soon he was gone, too. I watched as Grandma turned the savory meat over in the skillet and boiled the fat noodles in another pot.

"Grandma, do you realize by the time I'm twelve I'll be the only girl in the sixth grade in Morgan School going steady with a boy?"

Grandma stopped what she was doing.

"So you said, Betsi darling. And you also said that he

also doesn't know any of this yet." She turned to me. "Betsi, do you know that Grandma loves you?" she said seriously.

"Yes, Grandma, I do."

"Good, Betsi. Because I have a hard question to ask you. What if he doesn't want to go steady?"

I had never thought of that.

Chapter

SEVEN

Seven more days until twelve.
Day Five.

Dear Diary,

Oh, Diary, I want to get things started, and nothing has
happened so far. Saturday was wonderful, but now it's
Sunday. I've always hated Sundays. I called Tammy, and
she's out. Probably with her parents and little brother. It's
their family day. I called Kelly. She spends Sundays with
her father. Lisa and Lida always go to their grandmother's
on Sunday. Not only was today boring, boring, and boring, but—I'm nervous!

Will it really work, Di?

What will I do on Monday when I see Donny? See, I told a little white lie to the Double A's. As you know, I don't talk to Donny. I can't. But the Double A's don't know. I have had a crush on him, and I haven't said two words to him since September. Maybe I should have told them I had this problem.

Well, it's kind of a vanilla-pudding-colored day. Sundays are always like that for me. Chris listens to music. Abbie studies. Mom and Dad do some work. Grandma went to see her sister Esther in the Bronx. I would give today a 0 for no attendance. But tomorrow's Monday. I hope something happens.

Love and xxx's
Betsi with an *i*

Monday morning came sooner than I expected. It usually does. I found myself on the crosstown bus, staring out the window and feeling a new sensation. I wondered if I was sick. My stomach was jumping up and down and flipping and flopping. I usually didn't think twice about going to school on Monday. It was just something I had to do, like taking my vitamins. But this Monday was different. I had butterflies in my stomach. And I didn't like the feeling at all.

I dashed into school saying, "Hi, hi, hi," but not really knowing whom I was saying hello to. The first class I had was French. Donny was in my French class. Usually I looked forward to it, because Donny was a D and I was a P, so he was in the front and I was in the back. I liked to stare at his curly black hair. It looked like little black circles. The problem was I had spent all day Sunday daydreaming about Donny, so my mind hadn't been on my homework. Suddenly I prayed the teacher wouldn't call on me. What if I made a mistake? I'd die of embarrassment. It would be better if she didn't call on me at all.

I heard a voice whispering, "Betsi, Dunk is calling on you."

Ms. Dunkette is our French teacher. I could feel my cheeks burning hot. Not only did I not know the answer, I hadn't heard the question.

All I could see was Donny's curly black hair falling in his black eyes. He had turned around to look at me. I thought I'd die as I said, "Um, I didn't hear the question, Ms. Dunkette."

The next class was gym.

"I don't know how to talk to boys!" I blurted out to the Double A's while we were changing into our gym suits.

Tammy took charge. "Everyone meet in the library for study hall. By the biographies A–M. Okay?"

"We got kicked out of the library last week for talking too loud," Kelly said.

We couldn't talk in gym because we were too busy. After gym, we peeled off our gym suits and made a beeline for biographies. As we all trooped in we gave special smiles to the librarian with the big horn-rimmed glasses and pretty ruffly blouse.

"Look, I don't think I can do it. I thought I could, but I think I might have lied just a little bit. I mean, I think I should go steady to be special, but I don't know what to do."

"Do what?" Lisa said.

"Why are you getting so nervous?" Lida said.

"We'll figure it out for you," Tammy said.

"Girls," the librarian said. "It would be easier to keep your voices down if you'd read a biography. And it would be easier for the other students, too."

"We said we'd help you," Kelly said in a whisper.

"Then help me!" I wailed.

The librarian said loudly. "This is your last warning, girls."

"I'm thinking," Tammy said.

She was still thinking when we left the library and went into the cafeteria. Tammy was a heavy thinker. I took out the sandwich my mother had packed, and I swear it tasted like sawdust on cardboard.

Finally Tammy was through thinking. She made her important announcement. "There will be a meeting of the Double A's to consider your problem. Can it be at your house?"

That was it? That was what all the thinking was about?

"Sure," I said. "Chris broke his hand, so there won't be any piano playing. There should be quiet."

I slammed the door behind me, and my mom yelled from the living room, "Betsi, don't slam the door." She was sitting on the couch with a man who had a mustache that curled up at the ends. He wore a black beret and was holding a drawing pad on his lap.

"This is Sal, Betsi. He's the art director on my new assignment. This is Betsi, my middle child."

He looked up and smiled. "Hi, Betsi."

"What are you working on?" I asked.

"Oh, a new product," my mom said, her eyes shining. "It's a whipped cream that comes in all different flavors: strawberry, chocolate chip, banana, lemon, and piña colada."

"Yummy," I said. "A dessert on top of your dessert!"

Just then I heard hysterical crying coming from Abbie's room. I looked at my mom. "What's happened?"

"Oh, she'll be all right. She's been home since noon. The school put her in a cab."

"Gee, is she sick or something?" I really regretted the upswing in my voice.

"No," my mom said, her face pale. "She got a C minus on her sewing project."

I gasped. "Abbie got a grade other than an A? I don't believe it." Then I remembered the wrinkled plaid thing

71

with the crooked ruffle and the two ties, one a little shorter than the other, and I believed it. That apron was a mess. I could feel myself losing control of the muscles around my mouth, and I knew I had a slightly mean grin on my face. It wasn't nice, but I couldn't help it. "So what's she going to do? It will be on her report card. She won't have all As anymore."

My mom's forehead looked all wrinkled. "Well, she says she's going to hire a lawyer. Then she says she's going to stay in her room and take nothing but liquids. Betsi, can you do anything? There's nothing I can do to help her right now. I have all this work."

Sal turned big, brown, velvety, pleading eyes on me.

I shrugged and walked toward Abbie's room. It was going to be pretty hard to be nice when secretly I felt glad. I did hate myself for it, but in reality it was only a messed-up apron. So she wouldn't be a seamstress when she grew up. She had broken her record, and that must make her feel awful. She wasn't a legend in her own lifetime now, but she was still special.

I knocked on her door softly and whispered, "Abbie?" before opening it a crack. A stuffed animal came flying out at me and hit me on the head.

So much for Abbie. I tried. Besides, I had problems of my own, and the Double A's were coming over soon. I was just changing from my school uniform into my jeans when I heard wild screaming from the living room.

I realized it could only be the shrieking voice of my obnoxious little brother. When I came out he was standing with his shirttails hanging below his sweater, swinging his huge white cast around in circles and having a fit. I wondered then what my parents would say if I ever pulled the kind of stuff Chris and Abbie pulled. But I wasn't a genius.

"Lutzy left me!" Chris was screaming, his face red.

"Who's Klutzy?" Sal asked.

"Oh, his piano teacher, Klutzy. I mean Mr. von Lutz. Lutzy," my mom said, and I could tell she was really frazzled and very embarrassed. The whipped cream job was important to her. "Chris is a child prodigy. He was practicing for a recital at Carnegie Hall when he broke his hand," she explained to Sal, who still looked a little confused.

Then she turned to Chris. "Darling, Lutzy didn't leave you. Lutzy loves you. It's just that there's no reason for him to come if you're not taking lessons. You understand, darling. Now go into the kitchen and have some cookies and milk so I can work. Okay, darling?"

With that my precious, precocious little brother took his foot with his dirty sneaker and kicked the wall. He wasn't just an average brat, he was a special child prodigy brat.

Sal reached in his pocket, and he swallowed two pills without water. I always wondered how people did that.

Chris went out of the room finally, and my mother explained to Sal what a trauma this was for him. The buzzer from down in the lobby sounded, and I ran to the speaker to listen. The doorman said solemnly that the Double A's were there, and should he send them up. I yelled back, "Okay, send them up!" Then I turned and noticed my mom, who looked like she was on the brink of a nervous breakdown.

"We're having a meeting this afternoon, Mom. It's very important, but I promise we'll be very quiet. I'll close the door to my room, and you won't even hear a peep."

The front doorbell rang then, and in trooped Tammy with her watermelon-slice dance bag bouncing against her hip. Kelly was in socks and sneakers and running shorts, and Lisa and Lida wore matching jeans and red tops and red socks. Their hair was braided identically.

You could still hear Abbie sobbing in her room, and Chris was in the kitchen banging drawers around angrily.

"What's with the two stars?" Tammy asked as we went to my room.

I said it as if I was bored. "Abbie got a C minus in sewing, and Chris thinks his piano teacher doesn't love him anymore."

"Wow," Tammy said. "A C minus, not even a C plus. What's she going to do now? She's ruined."

"Chris's teacher still loves him, it's just that he doesn't get paid anymore," Kelly said.

"Hey," I said. "Is this meeting about me or not?"

Lisa and Lida plopped down on my powder-blue bedspread, and each hugged a powder-blue throw pillow. Kelly sat on my powder-blue throw rug. And Tammy sat in my powder-blue wicker rocking chair and rocked.

I stood up and paced around. "Do you ever get tired of powder blue?" Tammy asked. "I think you need to make some changes. It takes a little effort to get a steady boyfriend."

"In six days," Kelly said.

"You should wear tighter jeans and tops," Lida said.

"And try a little makeup, just a little lipstick," Lisa added.

"I think you should find out what he likes to talk about," Kelly said.

"But I'm not talking to him!" I said, exasperated.

"You should smile at him so he knows you're interested," Tammy said.

Maybe they were right. I couldn't be a lump anymore. Running to my closet, I found tight, tight jeans and a bright hot-pink sweater that my grandma had knitted me when I was in the fourth grade. Changing immediately, I slipped into little heels and found a rose-pink lipstick, which I smeared across my face. I hated lipstick. It made me break out. Then I turned dramatically and stuck out my Double A chest, smiling broadly, and said in a sickeningly sweet voice (or at least that was how it sounded to me), "Donny, I've been sitting behind you in French since September, our lockers are opposite each other, and I think it's time we *talked*. Tell me, Donny, do you like baseball, football, basketball, beach ball, racketball, stickball, or what kind of ball *do* you like? My name's Betsi with an *i*, in case you haven't noticed, because you're D for Delbert and I'm P for Paulson. Would you like to go to the movies Friday night? Of course I'll pay."

Everyone cracked up and rolled on the floor, thumping their fists, gasping for breath, laughing a deep laugh that sounded like some sort of animal. But it helped me to do that because I had felt like a walking veggie since it was decided I would be going steady with Donny. Donny, to whom I talked only in my diary.

I heard Sal and my mom, and I hoped we weren't making too much noise. My mom stuck her head in the door. Then I heard her say to Sal, "They must be talking about sex. They always get giggly."

I heard Sal tell my mom, "You know, they say if just one child is normal, it's okay."

Actually I decided then that I didn't like my tight, tight jeans. I liked room to breathe. The sweater was itchy, and I should have given it to my little cousin a long time ago. As for makeup for school, my mom would never approve. Only on special occasions was I allowed to wear lipstick.

Suddenly I felt depressed.

I agreed that I needed to change—everybody needed to change for the better—but I needed help doing it. If I had until eighth grade, okay, but in six days? I think I needed a miracle.

Tammy was thinking the same thing. "It's not enough. We need something more."

"A lot more," Kelly said.

"Wait, I'm thinking," Tammy said. "And when I finish thinking Betsi and Donny will be going steady."

Chapter

EIGHT

"**W**ell?" Lisa and Lida said impatiently.

"Let's get this show on the road," Kelly said. Kelly did everything fast, which was why she was so good at sports.

I just sat there holding my breath and waiting for Tammy's plan. Finally I shouted, "What is it, already?"

Tammy was still thinking. So we waited.

"Okay, here's the plan. We need to have a party and invite all of the sixth grade. Boys and girls. Our first mixer."

"But?" I said.

"When are we having the party?" Lisa asked.

"Soon, real soon, maybe even in the middle of the week. We only have about a week to pull this off," Tammy said, concentrating.

Everyone nodded. Every day was a day less for me to go steady with Donny.

"But?" I said.

"We don't have much time," Kelly said. "We have to invite everyone and plan the food and—"

"But?" I said again.

"Just where are we having this party, anyway?" Lisa asked.

"Oh, no problem," Tammy said. "At my house. My parents like me to have my friends over. Besides, we have the largest living room. Now we have to make lists!" This was her favorite part.

"But!"

Tammy turned to me. "Yes, Betsi, what's the *but*? Don't you trust me?"

"How am I going to go steady with Donny in six days if all we do is throw a party?"

Tammy stood up. She was wearing a purple sweater over jeans and her curly hair was pulled back with a big purple clip.

"That's just the first part of the plan," she said, smiling slyly. "At the party you can get closer to Donny. I mean, how close can you get in French? Then you can invite him to dinner at your house. One thing will lead to another, and before you know it you'll be going steady. It'll be all over school in a flash!"

It was a good plan. All Tammy's plans were good. But this time I thought it was a little too good, too perfect. Like some very important pieces were missing.

"Yeah, but," Kelly said, "what if he can't go to dinner? We haven't got much time."

"Well, I think it's good," Lida said. "Just think how much more popular he would be if he was going steady."

He seemed pretty popular to me already.

"I like it," Lisa said. "Everything works better with a plan, and now we have one."

Tammy shook her head, and her purple clip fell on the powder-blue rug. As she picked it up she smiled and said, "There's more to it."

I glanced around my perfect powder-blue room and suddenly wondered what I had gotten myself into. Stuffed under my bed in a cardboard box were my Barbie dolls, which I still played with every once in a while. When I went steady with Donny would I have to throw them away?

"Listen, Betsi, what do you talk about with Donny? This is the key to how fast we can have you going steady."

I felt a large lump form in my throat. I should have told them before. "Once I said, 'Hi, Donny.' The other time I said, 'That was a hard test, huh, Ronny? I mean Donny.'"

Everyone looked at me.

"That's all you've ever said to him?" Kelly asked.

I'd have bet money that none of them had ever said more than that to Donny, either. I guess my how-to-be-special strategy would be off now. You can't go steady with someone you can't talk to. For some reason I thought my friends could make a miracle, and we could pull it off. But if the miracle involved my talking to him, it would be hard. And if it involved inviting him to dinner, that would be impossible. I would never be able to eat in front of Donny. I'd be afraid the food would just sit in my mouth and I wouldn't be able to chew.

Kelly had an I-told-you-so smile.

But Tammy had one of her one-more-trick-up-my-sleeve smiles. "Listen, Betsi," she said. "What *can* you talk about with Donny?"

I could feel everyone staring at me. "Not much" was all I said.

No one took her eyes off me.

"I—uh—I—I, uh, you know, don't say much. Donny's kind of quiet."

Lisa leaned back against her sister. Kelly fell flat on her back with her knees up. Tammy plopped down on the floor cross-legged.

So now it was out. I had never said much to Donny since September, when I realized I had a crush on him. I talked to all the other boys in my class, because they didn't matter—but never to Donny. At least not a complete sentence. I should have told everyone, but I wanted to be special so badly. I guessed the deal was off.

Then Tammy said, "Lisa, what do you talk to Donny about?"

"Huh? Well, we don't say much."

"And Lida?"

"Well, I have trouble talking to boys I have crushes on."

"Kelly, can you help Betsi?" Tammy asked.

"Maybe we should find a hobby for her for when she's twelve."

Then Kelly did an un-Kelly-like thing. She started giggling hysterically and then rolled around on the rug, helpless with infectious laughter. We all started laughing. There was nothing wrong with me. No one talked to Donny. We were all tongue-tied. We all had crushes on him. Probably every girl in the sixth grade did. He probably hadn't spoken to a single girl since school started. He probably thought we were all unfriendly.

Then I heard my wonderful sister shouting, "Shut up in there! You sound like a bunch of cackling chickens."

"What's wrong with sister dear now?"

"Nothing but that C minus in home ec."

Then they started talking about Abigail again and that got me mad. Even when she goofed up she was special. This meeting was supposed to be about me—and only me.

Tammy stood up and looked at her watch because she had to get to a ballet class. "Okay, I have an idea. We'll practice role-playing with Betsi, and then she can start to talk to Donny like a friend, and he'll like her."

We stared at her.

"What's role-playing?" Kelly said. Sometimes it was hard to keep up with Tammy.

"My dad taught me how to do it when he was out of work," Tammy said. "He was selling shoes, and he wasn't doing very well until he learned role-playing. It works. You rehearse what you're going to say first, and then the other person can only say a few things in response, and then you make the sale."

"But what if it doesn't work that way?" Kelly said. "I mean, what if Betsi rehearses one thing to say, and Donny says a whole bunch of other things, and she doesn't know what to say next? What if she's standing there with her tongue dangling out of her mouth?"

"That's how I feel," I shouted. "How did you know what it was like?"

Kelly blushed.

Tammy shook her head and stamped her turned-out feet. "Why are you all so negative? This is a real challenge to the Double A's, and when you have a real challenge you have to try a little harder."

Tammy stood at one side of my powder-blue dresser.

"Listen, here's how it works. I'm going to pretend to be you. Hi, Donny. We're having a party. Are you coming?"

Then she ran over to the other side of the dresser near my powder-blue chair with the powder-blue throw pillow and pretended to be Donny.

"Gee, Betsi, that sounds great! When is it, and what should I bring?"

Tammy threw the ball to me. "Okay, now what would you say?"

"I'd say the party is soon"—when was the party? —"and tell him what to bring."

"That's not the idea," Tammy said as if I were a Neanderthal girl. "The idea is to start a conversation."

"Say the first thing that comes into your mind," Kelly whispered.

"Hi, Donny," I said as if I were a wind-up toy. "Do you want some grape bubble gum?"

"Very good," Tammy said, moving around the room as if she was a director. "Can you do anything else with that? Like say that your favorite flavor is grape, or that you love bubble gum—does he? Or go on to ask him how he did on his French test."

The Double A's were watching with their mouths open. See, Tammy did know how to do this, but if she was so good at it, why wasn't *she* going steady with Donny?

84

Sometimes I wished I could be as clever as Tammy. But the thing was that Tammy sometimes got us all in a lot of trouble, too.

Suddenly I got it!

"Donny, we're having a party Wednesday, Thursday, or Friday, and I was wondering if you could bring the cheese dip, the cheese, or the Cheez Doodles."

With that the twins and Kelly fell all over one another chuckling. Tammy, who was trying to play teacher, laughed and bent in half like she had cramps.

"That was good, Betsi," Tammy said. "See, at least you talked."

"But that wasn't Donny," Kelly protested. "That was just us playing around."

Suddenly Tammy got out her list. "Listen, we have to have the party fast. Because of our timetable. It will have to be Thursday."

"Not Friday? Friday is party night," Lisa said.

"But we've never had a mixed party. So it could be Thursday. Everyone would come. Besides, we could have it from six-thirty to eight-thirty. That would be okay," Lida said.

We all took lists and wrote what had to be done. I had only six days left, which meant the party should have been two weeks earlier.

I wondered if anyone would come.

Dear Diary,

Four days to go until twelve.
Day Eight.

Dear Diary,

Oh, I said that already. I guess I didn't feel like writing in you last night or Monday night. Something really strange happened around here after dinner last night, Di. My dad announced that we were going to have a family meeting. At first it sounded great, because I knew Tammy's family meets every Sunday night, and they talk about sex education. I hoped it would be that, but it wasn't about that.

I sure wished I felt as close to my dad as I do to my mom. My dad's a psychologist, and sometimes I think he sees us as if we were specimens for him to examine in a big glass fishbowl.

"Chris," my dad said, "how did you feel about Abigail getting a C minus in sewing?"
Chris was astonished. "I didn't even know she had. Wow, a grade less than an A. That's impossible."

My dad's very clever. Of course Chris didn't know, because he was worried about his precious hand, and Abbie didn't really care about Chris's hand after her initial concern because she was having a heart attack about her less-than-A catastrophe.

86

Finally my dad turned to me and smiled. "And, Betsi, what do you think?"

See, there was a perfect chance, Diary, to say what I really thought. That I felt I was unspecial. That I needed to be special by my twelfth birthday. That I was this nerdy middle child. But then I saw my dad looking at his watch, and I knew he had to go back to his office for his evening patients.

Instead I said, "Well, Daddy, I think I have to do my homework. I think Abigail should try to get A pluses and that Chris should find a hobby while he can't play the piano. Something he doesn't have to do with his hands. Like jogging."

My father slapped himself on his thigh and chuckled, saying, "Leave it to Betsi." My mom beamed at me

But I had the feeling that nothing was really said. Like how come the family meeting had to be about Chris and Abbie? Abbie would still get into Yale or Harvard. And Chris's piano playing would probably be better after he rested. When the cast came off and Lutzy came back he would have his recital with rave reviews.

But the thing, Diary, that made me feel bad is that he didn't say, "And how are you, Betsi? Do you have any problems?"

It's always been like that.

I feel invisible in this family.

I really needed that, Di. Today is crucial. I have to talk. I really have to say something intelligent to Donny today. I have to invite him to the party and make conversation and begin to be friends with him so he'll get the idea that he wants to go steady with me.

On to today, DD, and wish me luck. I hope Tammy's role-playing pays off, because now I like Donny even more. I think it will be a bright orange day with powder-blue stripes. A nice B+ day. Now that's positive thinking.

What do you think, Di?

Chapter

NINE

It took us a half hour to invite all of the sixth grade to the party at Tammy's on Thursday night. When they found out it was a boy–girl party they all wanted to come. It didn't matter that it was a weeknight. Anyway, it would end early.

Tammy had lists of what everyone was bringing. She had lists of parents who would take groups of kids who lived near one another in cabs. We had lists of our lists. Of course, my mind was as far away from school as it could be. My whole future depended on this party and what would happen at it.

I got scared and couldn't talk to Donny in French class.

All I did was stare at his curly black hair, trying to figure out when he should get a haircut. I had planned to walk out the door with him, but some other girl did.

It was in the hall that it happened, and it was like a miracle. I found my voice, and it wasn't high and squeaky or anything. I said, "Donny, we're having a party tomorrow night, and I was wondering if you could come."

He smiled at me. "Oh, yeah, I heard. The whole class will be there. I'm supposed to bring green olives." Green olives? How could I take that further? I couldn't. So I said, "Well, listen, I'll see you at the party. It should be lots of fun." I could have said, "Save a dance for me." I could have said, "How are you doing in French?" I could have said, "You can bring black olives if you want," but he had walked away.

When he had looked at me and smiled I thought I would melt into a puddle. Maybe he did like me—just a little.

I was feeling silly and giddy. I couldn't have said anything intelligent for money, and my stomach felt as if it was on a roller coaster. But what I hated most was the feeling in my knees. It felt as if I had lost control of them and my body.

While I was in that state a lot of girls began to circulate around me. They were looking at me as if I was their new leader.

"Betsi, can I bring pretzels instead of cheese dip? It's easier."

"Uh-huh" was all I could manage.

"Betsi, is it true everyone's wearing jeans?"

"Uh-huh."

"Betsi, I have to know that there will be cabs to take us home. My mom's very strict about that."

"Uh-huh."

Finally I caught up with Tammy, who had so many lists she had safety-pinned some of them to her sweater. We were walking together against the general tide of traffic. Morgan is much smaller than a public school, but they somehow pack more people in because a lot of parents want their kids to go there.

"I talked to him, Tammy," I said, feeling my cheeks flush.

"What did he say?"

"I don't remember, but he's coming, and he's bringing olives."

Tammy checked her list and said, "Right. Donny Delbert, olives." She ruffled through her lists again. "Did he say much?"

"He smiled."

"But he didn't say much?" Tammy seemed happy. I wondered what was on her mind now. "That's a good sign. That means he has trouble talking to you, too. Boys are a lot like girls in that way. They find it hard to talk to girls when they like them. He probably has a crush on you." Then she walked away. I stood there hugging my books and wondering if Tammy was right.

* * *

When I got home from school that afternoon the doorman took a folded note out of his pocket. I was in such a fog about Donny that I had forgotten about my grandma! Quickly I unraveled the note—this time written on bright red paper with a blue Magic Marker.

Betsi,

Grandma loves you.

Uh-oh. It was Wednesday now. I began to feel very guilty that I hadn't seen her since Saturday. Walking fast, I passed our bank of elevators and walked to the end of the hall and waited, tapping my foot, for her elevator to come.

I buzzed our secret signal at her door, and my grandma answered immediately. Grandma was always there for me. I don't know why I had forgotten her. No, actually I hadn't. All I could think of was Donny.

"It's me," I said, and Grandma gave me a big hug and a kiss. "Come in and tell me everything. You must be busy."

The living room was neat and sparkling as usual. Grandma had pink, white, and red carnations in a vase on the coffee table now. I twitched my nose. "Chocolate chip cookies?"

She nodded. Then I had a thought. Hey, what about

strawberry chip cookies—but, no. It was too late now, and I had a new plan. Donny for dinner.

Grandma picked up her knitting. She had three balls going at once, yellow, red, and blue. "It's a new design," she said proudly. "I invented it. Comes out like little flowers." She looked at me over her glasses, which kept slipping down her nose. "So how's school?"

I shrugged. "Oh, it's okay," I said, watching her knit. I couldn't tell her the real truth. I'd be ashamed. Half the time I didn't take my brain to school. All I could think about was Donny, Donny, Donny.

"So how's the boyfriend?" she asked, studying me.

"Abbie got a C minus in sewing," I said.

"Well, she'll survive it," Grandma said, putting her knitting down. "I'm a lousy sewer, too."

"And Chris is having tantrums because Lutzy isn't back," I said quickly.

"His hand will heal."

I nodded. She nodded back. Then she went to the kitchen and brought back a plate of gooey, melty, crunchy, munchy cookies.

"Does Abbie have a boyfriend?" Grandma asked. I giggled. What a question.

"Did you go steady, Grandma, when you were a girl?"

Grandma laughed and kept knitting. "Oh, yes, we did everything you young people do. Only when we went steady it was usually serious. We usually ended up getting married."

"How old were you when you married Grandpa Lester?" I bit into another cookie, and we were quiet for a minute in his memory.

"Oh, I was just sixteen. Not much older than our Abigail. But you see, in those days it was the Great Depression, and it was better for a girl to be married. College was out of the question for most girls."

Wow, I thought, having a revelation. If I was patient and waited a few years, we could marry off Abbie, and that would get her out of the house forever. But it was no good. Abbie would definitely go to college and be home on vacations.

"So how's the boyfriend?"

I never knew why I couldn't lie to my grandma or that she wouldn't let me lie to her.

"Oh, Grandma," I blurted out, "he doesn't even talk to me, and when I try to talk to him I can't."

"Always be yourself, Betsi."

I looked at her knitting and began to see the little flowers. Grandma was so creative. I had sixteen sweaters that had her labels: Smart Cookie.

"Do you think you should let him in on it, that you're going to be going steady with him? I know they do things differently now, but—"

"Well, we have a plan—the Double A's." I leaned in closer to her. "The plan is to have a party, and then at the party I'll ask him to dinner, and then from there—"

Grandma interrupted me. "Dinner at your house?"

"Well, yeah."

"I wonder if that's such a good idea, Betsi. As much as I love everyone—well, it is a pretty lively family."

My grandma always puts things in such a nice way.

"In my day girls didn't do exactly what you're doing. We would set our cap for someone, and then we would plan strategies to be where they were. Then again, maybe you should make him jealous."

"Of whom?"

"I see your point," she said, changing rows. I watched the little colored balls bounce around. "Maybe you could get in some sort of trouble, and he'd have to help you out."

"I am in trouble. He's the trouble."

"I see your point."

I looked around the room—it was so pretty and restful. Grandma's favorite color was peach. The sofa was peach, the sofa blanket she had knitted was peach, and there was a peach-colored bowl with ripe peaches in it. On the cabinet the clock said it was almost five-thirty. I had planned to spend some extra time on my homework that night to try to give my life some semblance of sanity.

"Grandma?" I asked. "Do you role-play?"

"No, a little gin rummy is all I play. But you could learn, you're young still."

I kissed her good-bye, and she walked me to the door, still knitting. As I went out I kissed her again and asked, "Why don't you come down to our apartment, Grandma?"

"Oh, I don't want to impose," she said.

I rode down in the elevator deep in thought, and as I crossed over to our elevators I thought they should carve out a shortcut to my grandma's apartment.

Things were sure different since Chris didn't have his daily lessons. It was quiet. When I got in the front door my mom was in the living room wearing her baseball cap and her "Munsen's Marmalade" T-shirt.

I plopped my books on the couch and took off my blazer.

"Where were you, Betsi? I have some ad copy for you to help me with."

"Oh, up at Grandma's. She made chocolate chip cookies."

"Why doesn't she come down more? It seems like we hardly ever see her. I could call, but I don't want to impose."

Grownups. At this rate no one would see anyone.

"What are you working on, Mom?"

"I'm working on some slogans for a new flavor of licorice."

"A new flavor besides strawberry?"

"Lemon licorice!"

"Wow! How about 'Try a new twist'? Or you could call it citrus licorice. Or you could call it the Big Yellow. Or 'If you hate licorice, you'll love new Lemon Licorice.' "

"I'm going to get writer's cramp, Betsi, trying to keep up with you. How do you think so fast? I'm always so slow."

I loved to do this with my mom.

But then Abbie slammed the door. "Mom, I didn't get an A plus on the English test."

"That's all right, dear. Keep trying."

Then Chris walked through the front door grinning. He hadn't done that in a long time. My dad had taken some time off from work to go shopping with him. Chris held up a big plastic bag from a sporting goods store. "Jogging equipment," he said. Nice of him to thank me for my idea, but he probably forgot. He disappeared into his room.

"Mom?" I said while the coast was clear. "We're having our first boy–girl party tomorrow night at Tammy's. The whole sixth grade is coming. I'm supposed to bring three bags of nacho tortilla chips."

I thought my mom was going to cry. "Oh, Betsi, your first party with boys. Listen, it's not too late. Let's run out and buy you a new dress. Oh, this is so exciting, isn't it?"

"Mom, no. All the girls are wearing jeans. It's just casual. Really, no one's mother is rushing out to buy her a dress."

She looked disappointed.

My dad must have been listening because he came in then and put his arm around her and said, "Listen,

Maggie, a new dress is what they did in your day. If Betsi wants to wear jeans, then she should."

"My little Betsi is growing up," my mom said.

"Well, it sounds great," my dad said. "I wouldn't mind going to the party myself."

"Oh, you are, Daddy. You're a parent group leader. What you have to do is take five kids who live near our apartment home in a cab. Can you be at Tammy's at eight-thirty tomorrow?"

My mom clapped her hands and said, "I love it. I just love it."

Then Abigail came waltzing in and sat on the arm of my dad's black recliner. "Father, dear, I've decided what I want to be when I grow up."

If she ever did—grow up, that is. Abigail was the moodiest person I knew. One minute she was down in the dumps and the next minute ready to conquer the world.

"I'm going to be a doctor," she announced.

"I'm very impressed, Abigail," my dad said.

Sure, I thought. Dr. Abigail Paulson. She'd do it, too, and she'd be one better than my dad, who was a doctor, too, but only a Ph.D.

Chris came into the room lugging his tape recorder with his good hand. "Look what I found! The tape Lutzy made of me playing at Carnegie Hall at eight. Liszt's Hungarian Rhapsody No. 2. Anyone want to hear it as played by Christopher Paulson two years ago?"

"How could I say no? You know it's my favorite," my mom said. But I sensed she wanted to get back to work.

"So, Dad," I said. Everyone looked up at me. Chris was lying on his stomach, fiddling with the recorder. Abigail was still sitting on the arm of my dad's favorite black chair. Mom was sitting on the couch.

"I need to know for sure that you'll take the kids home from the party in a cab at eight-thirty."

"Oh, sure," he said absentmindedly. "It'll be fine." He was watching Chris insert a cassette.

"Oh, the sixth grade is having a boy-girl party. I heard about that," Abbie said acidly. "What is it? Forty children in one living room? My, my, I just love intimate parties. It should resemble a gym."

"Shhh, it's starting," Chris said, awed by his own playing.

"Why such short notice?" my mom asked me suddenly. "I mean, it's tomorrow night." The thing about mothers, they never miss a beat, and mine was no exception.

I shrugged. "Oh, we just planned it that way. You see, the reason we did that was—"

"Shhhh," Chris was saying. The first part of the tape was crashing applause as they introduced the young Christopher Paulson. Chris jumped to his feet and bowed from the waist.

Everyone applauded. I still thought it was just to make him feel better.

"We invited a purple and green Martian, and he has to leave by Saturday. He's making a stopover in Venus. That's why the party's tomorrow."

"That's nice, dear," said my mom, but no one was really listening. They were listening to Chris's tape.

I walked back to my room, not because I didn't want to hear Chris, but because I had a mad desire to write in my diary. The only problem was that I had already written in it that day. But I decided there was no law against writing twice.

Day Eight almost over.
Four days left till I'm twelve.

Diary,

I go around pretending I'm happy, but I feel really confused. It's like I've lost control of my life. Like I'm not Betsi with an *i* anymore. Everything's different now. Before I used to wake up and it would be a new, exciting day. Now it's pressure, pressure, pressure.

I had this quiet crush on Donny, but now he's the one who's going to make me special. And this is my last chance. Because you're only twelve once. And now there's a deadline, and it's making me nervous.

The thing was, before I was unspecial and unhappy, but now that we have this plan I feel only nervous. I day-dream all the time. Sometimes I wonder if I have a brain.

Strike that, Diary. I'm being ungrateful.

The Double A's are my very best friends in the world, and Tammy is brilliant. They would never let me down. I should stop being nervous. They're giving me a chance to be special.

Today was kind of a blue- and red- and yellow-colored yarn day. I just know everything's going to work out, and tomorrow will be powder blue. I'd give today a C minus, but tomorrow will have a much higher grade.

Love and xxx's
Betsi with an *i*

Chapter

TEN

I thought I'd never make it through school on Thursday. After school I did my homework in record-breaking time, and it looked it, too. Then I spent an hour deciding on a casual peach-colored top and some old jeans. Then I went over to Tammy's to help set up.

When she opened the door my first words were "Oh, no."

She was wearing a blue skirt, white angora sweater, and black flats.

"Everyone's supposed to wear jeans," I said rather loudly.

"I know." She shrugged. "Don't worry, they will. It's just that my mom wanted me to dress up because it's at my house, and I'm kind of the hostess. I would have loved to have worn jeans."

Then she whispered, "My dad's staying around for the party. I wish he wouldn't, but he said he wouldn't miss it for the world." It might not be so bad having a famous soap opera star passing out potato chips. I didn't know Tammy's father very well.

The doorbell rang. It was Lisa and Lida holding a bag of cheese and crackers. When they took off their raincoats I could see they were wearing matching red dresses.

"I thought we were all wearing jeans!"

"Everyone is " Lisa said. "Don't worry."

"Mom insisted we wear these," Lida said. "When we got home from school she had put these new dresses on our beds. What could we do? We were going to wear jeans."

I looked down at my scruffy jeans and groaned. There was no chance to run home and change. Maybe they were right. Everybody else would wear jeans.

The doorbell rang again, and this time some boys came in. They looked more dressed up than they did in school. The doorbell rang like popcorn popping, and at six-fifteen all of the sixth graders were standing in Tammy's big living room looking at one another.

I was the only girl wearing jeans.

At the last minute everyone, or everyone's mother, had changed her mind. I felt as if I'd been betrayed. I wanted to go home, but the party was for me.

Before I had a chance to find Tammy, Donny walked through the door. He was immediately surrounded by a bunch of boys. In fact, the boys stood on one side of the living room and the girls on the other.

There was wall-to-wall food on the dining room table, but no one was eating anything. Finally I signaled Tammy through the crowd. She turned on the record player. When the music blared through the crowded room some of the girls started dancing with other girls, and I saw Donny off to the side just watching. He was wearing a powder-blue turtleneck and a navy blazer, and I started to walk over to him, but I was intercepted by Tammy's father, Mr. Weinstock, who was carrying wooden bowls of potato chips and pretzels and serving everyone.

"Hi, Betsi. I'm Tammy's father under all this makeup. Perhaps you've seen me on TV. Have something to eat. There's plenty of food. Don't be shy."

He certainly wasn't. He had dressed up in a rented clown outfit with a crazy red wig, a bulbous nose, and rouged cheeks. There were balloons streaming up from his ruffled collar, and he was talking in a high, squeaky voice.

Tammy came up to me. "I could die of embarrassment. I could just die. He's doing this because
he could never afford a really terrific birthday party
for me when I was a kid."

"But this isn't your birthday!"

"I know. But you know my father's a little
strange."

I tried to get over to talk to Donny, but every
time I tried Mr. Weinstock got in the way. (Of
course, his acting name isn't Weinstock—it's Palmer.
Peter Palmer.) Now was my chance to talk to Donny.
But I saw some kids disappear into the bedroom—
Donny, too. I went in. It was my chance to talk to
him, because everyone was just sitting around.

"Gee, it's weird to have a lot of the sixth grade sitting
in my room," Tammy said.

I glanced over at Donny. He was sitting on the other
side of the room, and there was no way I could get
closer to him. He was already surrounded by tons of girls.
Funny, but wherever I was he was always on the other
side of the room.

I think it got started when Josh, who was the class
smart aleck, said "Hey, let's play spin the bottle."

The whole room became deadly silent. Then someone
giggled nervously. We wouldn't do it, of course.

As I watched the faces in Tammy's bedroom they
went in and out of focus. Most of the girls were smirk-

ing, and some of the boys were blushing. We weren't going to do this.

But it was Tammy who leapt up and dumped a pen and two pencils out of the vintage Coca Cola bottle on top of her desk. We had the bottle. It was no joke. I thought this was something you did in the seventh grade.

Someone grabbed the Coke bottle and spun it around so it stopped in front of Cheryl, who clapped her hand over her mouth and giggled.

"What do I do?"

"Spin the bottle," Eric said.

We were doing this, actually playing spin the bottle, I thought. I had never kissed a boy. I was still trying to talk to one.

She twisted it in her fingers, shut her eyes, and I watched wide-eyed as it landed in front of someone we had on our lists of possible boyfriends for me.

"Kiss Todd," someone whispered.

Cheryl looked over at Todd. All the boys were laughing and punching him.

"Maybe we shouldn't do this," Kelly said. "I mean, your mother and father are right here. What if they came in while we were kissing?"

I know when the Double A's had talked about kissing boys, Kelly had said she wasn't ready. I knew she must be terrified that the bottle would land in front of her.

"We can kiss in the bathroom. Then it'll look like we had to go," Eric said.

Todd and Cheryl gave him a dirty look.

"I don't want to do this in the bathroom," Cheryl said.

"Okay, in the closet," Tammy said. I couldn't believe how much she was into it.

When we planned the party we had never figured on anything like this. More kids came in the door to see what was going on. They were stopped at the door by a guard.

Cheryl and Todd disappeared into the closet. No one told us what to do when they were in there. Donny was looking at the ceiling. No one really looked at anyone else.

When they came out of the closet Cheryl blinked a little from the overhead light, but Todd was smirking.

Todd sat down on his knees and gave the bottle a spin. When it stopped at Jessica I could see his face light up. Jessica was in another girls' club in school and was tall and big for her age. She was also very pretty. When they disappeared into the closet we shut the door.

Suddenly I began to get scared. What if I didn't get a turn? I had never been kissed by a boy except for my cousin Michael, who kissed me at a family party. It felt like a wet sponge.

"What if their braces get stuck together?" someone said. They both did have braces on their upper teeth.

People were looking at their watches when Jessica and Todd went into the closet. After about thirty seconds someone picked up the Coke bottle and made loud smacking sounds against it with his lips. Everyone giggled.

"That's disgusting," I heard Kelly say. She must have been feeling really panicky and wishing it would be over. Kissing games just weren't Kelly.

Then out of the closet came Todd and Jessica. Everyone applauded. Todd had a big rose imprint of a lip on his lips. And Jessica looked like someone had taken cold cream and smeared it across her mouth.

Then it got to be routine. The only thing that wasn't routine was what was happening to Kelly. She looked like she was ready to cry. Then I noticed the bottle. It was slowing down and was going to end up pointing at Kelly. I was sitting right next to her, so I half shoved her out of the way so the bottle would aim at me.

Howard? I was going to go into that dark closet and kiss Howard? Howard's breath smelled like dill pickles.

We went into the dark closet and stood there while Howard made a little kissing noise in the air. We came out hand in hand, as if it was the most wonderful experience we had ever had.

I sat down on my knees and spun the bottle and heard

four loud but recognizable gasps as it landed smack in front of a certain dark-haired boy in a powder-blue turtleneck and a navy blazer. Donny. My knees felt weak. I had to kiss Donny.

I took a deep breath and stood up. Hadn't I day-dreamed about this for a long time? My fantasy was coming true. In the closet I bumped into Tammy's terry bathrobe and got entangled in it. For a second I fumbled around in the dark. I thought I'd die of embarrassment, but then I felt his lips press gently against mine. It was heavenly. I was blushing when we went out of the closet, and I kept my eyes down. What I saw first was a monstrous pair of clown shoes. Then I looked up and up and saw Mr. Weinstock with his sad clown face. Every-one knew he knew. I knew he knew I had been in the closet with Donny, kissing.

Quietly we went single file out of the bedroom with Mr. Weinstock leading us. After that the bedroom was out of bounds—it had been quarantined. No more kiss-ing games was the message we got.

Back in the living room the music went on, and we continued to dance, but it wasn't the same for me. I felt my face would be permanently red, and I wanted to die of humiliation. Actually most people looked as if they felt awkward.

Mrs. Weinstock was slicing up some chocolate cake she had baked and putting it on paper plates. Just what I needed—gooey chocolate cake.

"Can we talk?" I whispered in Tammy's ear.

She was near tears. "I'm sorry he came in. He's so embarrassing. Did you get to talk to Donny?"

Talk to Donny? How could I ask him to dinner after we'd been caught coming out of a dark closet together?

But I had to do it. I knew I had to do it. Frantically I searched for him, and as usual he was on the other side of the room.

Then I thought I would be deaf as a whistle blew right near my ear. Mr. Weinstock was standing on a high-backed chair.

"Listen up, boys and girls. I hope you had a good time at our party." (At whose party?) "But all good things have to come to an end. The parent group leaders are waiting downstairs to take you home in cabs." He then proceeded to read from the lists.

I tuned out as he read the names for the cabs.

Lida ran up to me just then. "Listen, it's unfortunate what happened, but we pulled some strings. *You and Donny are riding in the same cab together!*"

"Now you have to ask him to dinner, Betsi. No excuses," Lisa said.

No excuses. I could think of some.

We waited in our groups while the elevators went down full and came up empty. Then our group squeezed into the elevator, and I was shoulder to shoulder with him. Maybe he felt embarrassed, too, but I couldn't ask him in front of everyone else.

When we got out of Tammy's apartment building I saw my dad waiting on the corner. There were five kids to a cab, and when he read his list he asked, "Where's Melissa?"

"She went in another cab," I said. "At the last minute they put Donny in our cab."

All the kids sat in the backseat, and my dad sat in the front. It was dark in the cab, and I ended up, not entirely by accident, sitting right next to Donny—our knees almost touching.

Then I forced myself to forget the closet and remember the role-playing, and I said, "So, Donny, did you like the party?" Now that was hard, because he had to forget the closet incident, too.

"Yeah, the party was great. I loved the chocolate cake."

He ate the chocolate cake? After what happened to us? By then I'd had it. I just had to plunge in. "Well, if you like chocolate cake, then maybe you'd want to come over for dinner. My mom makes great chocolate cake."

"Yeah? When?"

"Tomorrow night," I said, holding my breath.

"Tomorrow night sounds great," he said. I told him where I lived and what time to come and prayed he wouldn't change his mind.

"That'd be great, Betsi, because my mom's in Florida

111

visiting my grandmother. And to tell you the truth, my dad's not such a great cook."

He was coming, and we were talking. And tomorrow night was going to happen for real.

The cab dropped each kid off. When Donny got out of the cab I said, "Good-bye, Donny. I'll see you tomorrow night at six-thirty."

I had done it! I was so excited when the cab dropped me and my dad off that I kept jumping up and down on the sidewalk.

"Oh, Daddy," I said, hugging my father. "I like this boy, and I asked him to dinner, and he's coming."

"See, Betsi, that's what comes of being assertive. It's just as important for girls to be assertive as it is for boys, you know."

Wait—until—the—Double A's—found—out—about—this!

"Betsi," he said, "of all my children you're always so busy and involved. I hardly get to talk to you. But I'm happy for this moment we can share." He hugged me. "Remember, always be in touch with your feelings." One feeling I had was would it be okay for Donny to come over tomorrow?

Dear Diary,

Three days to go until twelve. Today is Day Nine.

I almost didn't make it, Di. First I was the only girl in jeans, then I couldn't find Donny. He was always on the other side of the room. Looking great as usual.

Then we played spin the bottle. I think half the couples never even kissed. But I did kiss Donny. It was great until we went out of the closet and Mr. Weinstock saw us coming out.

But I know that Donny must like me because he did kiss me. So I'm halfway there already. *And* he's coming to dinner tomorrow night. Tomorrow I should be going steady with Donny.

Today was a bright-red-trimmed-with-gold-brass-buttons day, and I would give it an A+ because finally Donny and I talked, but then there was Mr. Weinstock, so I'm going to have to give it a B+.

Chapter

ELEVEN

My mom said yes! We could have a boy for dinner, and we could have chocolate cake. It was way too late for me to tell the news to Tammy, Lisa, Lida, or Kelly. But I could tell Abigail.

As I went down the hall I saw the door was open to my sister's peppermint-pink bedroom. Everything was shades of pink, even the doors.

"Abbie!" I said excitedly as she was brushing her hair. "You'll never guess who's coming to dinner tomorrow night."

"I don't want to guess. I don't like guessing."

"Okay, it's Donny Delbert!"

Her head snapped around, and she dropped her pink hairbrush.

"Who?"

"Donny Delbert. I asked him to dinner, and he's coming."

"But he likes Felicity Grimes."

Leave it to Abbie to deflate me this way. Felicity Grimes was in the eighth grade!

Where was this unwritten law that sisters had to torture each other?

"Not many people know about it," Abbie shouted after me as I left her room in a hurry. "But I'm pretty sure it's true. He likes older girls."

I had walked away from her all-pink room toward my powder-blue room.

I got ready for bed and was climbing in when I saw my mom standing in the doorway.

"It was a big night for you, Betsi, huh?"

I wanted to say, "Yeah, I half kissed the most popular boy in my class in a dark closet, but I could never say that."

"Well, there will be more to come," she said, kissing me.

God. I hoped I'd be able to kiss a boy again.

As my mom was leaving my room I said, "Mom?"

"Yes, Betsi, dear?"

"Promise me there won't be any mistakes when Donny comes over to dinner."

"Mistakes? Why, Betsi, don't be silly. What could go wrong?"

*   *   *

When I told the Double A's they jumped up and down with me. The shouting was still ringing in my ears. I had almost made it to the final countdown. Then they gave me advice.

Tammy: "Talk about what you know. Stick to safe subjects. Like that he likes chocolate cake."

Kelly: "Eat slowly. Chew your food thirty-two times and swallow so you won't choke. And also talk a lot."

Lisa and Lida: "Don't wear jeans."

On the crosstown bus I felt as if I was floating. It was going to work, I knew it. I had already forgotten about Abbie. I smiled at the doorman, and when I turned my key in the apartment lock I smelled this fragrant roast beef aroma. My mom had started everything. That was great.

"Hey, Mom, I'm home!" I said. I said it again, but there was no answer. I ran to her little office. I ran all over the apartment. Panicking, I ran back to the kitchen table, and that's where I saw it.

Betsi,

I had an emergency appointment with Schwartz, O'Brien, Macaroni, and Whitehead. I'll be back soon. Don't worry.

What could go wrong? In this house? Everything.
I went into my room ready to face the three-hour-long

process of deciding what to wear. First I took everything out of my closet and put it on my bed. Then I heard a noise and looked up. Abbie was standing in my doorway. "Do you think I should wear this top to dinner?" she asked me.

I shrugged. Why was she so concerned about what top she was wearing for dinner? He'd be looking at me.

I told her not to wear the tight red sweater she had on because red was a bad color for her. She changed into a lime-green top with long sleeves. I told her it looked much better, but it didn't really. It was an old trick of mine.

"Don't wear jeans." Okay, I wouldn't. I picked out a blue velvet full skirt and a white satin blouse with a lace collar and little blue heels. Just as I was admiring myself in the mirror the phone rang.

"Betsi, it's for you," Abbie screeched.

Well, that was it. Donny was chickening out.

But he wasn't. It was my mother who was chickening out. "Oh, Betsi," she said, "I feel terrible about this, but I have to work late. I can't finish dinner. I won't even be there to eat dinner."

For the first time ever I felt angry at my mother's career—and her apologies for it. This was the most important night of my life. It was meant to determine my future.

117

"One thing you could do is order Kentucky Fried Chicken for tonight, and I'll reheat the roast for tomorrow night. You can switch nights and tell him to come then."

"Tomorrow will be too late, Mom," I said. Then I exclaimed that he was going on a vegetarian diet, but I knew that my mom wasn't listening anyway.

"What can we do?" she said.

"Grandma," I said.

"Oh, Betsi, I don't think you should impose on Grandma."

"Mom, I think she likes to be imposed on. I really do. She lives all alone."

"Okay, then," my mom said, clearly dying to get off the phone. "If she can finish dinner and serve it, you can have him over tonight. If not, I think you have to postpone it."

But I couldn't postpone it. I'd miss my deadline.

And I couldn't just call Grandma. That would be disrespectful. No time for a note that said, "Betsi loves you." I ran out the door. Breathless, I arrived at Grandma's door and pressed the doorbell, forgetting our special signal.

"Betsi, how nice you look."

"Oh, Grandma, Donny, the boy I'm supposed to go steady with, is coming to dinner tonight, and Mom has to work late, and Abigail doesn't know how to make chocolate cake, and—"

My grandma grabbed her bag. "Of course, Betsi, I'll make dinner. But are you sure I won't be imposing?"

I grabbed her hand, and we both ran for the elevator. Then we dashed through the lobby and waited for the other elevator, and then we waited for it to go up before dashing down the hall.

At about a quarter after six, the kitchen smelled like dinner was cooking. Grandma was just frosting the cake when Abbie strolled in.

"Why, Abigail, how nice you look," Grandma said.

I didn't think so. She had changed back into the tight red sweater, and she was wearing shiny red lipstick.

Then the door slammed, and my dad came into the kitchen and kissed my grandma. "Mother, I'm glad you could come to dinner."

"Mom's tied up at a business meeting, and we're having company for dinner," I said. "Grandma's making dinner"

"Oh, yes, that boy."

"Donny," Abbie and I said together accidentally.

The doorbell rang. There was only one person it could be.

He was early. I wasn't ready. I looked around for a place to hide. Grandma gave me a little squeeze and a hug. "Don't worry, Betsi. It'll be fine. Just have fun. After all, what could go wrong?"

My dad went to answer the door, and I realized he had changed into jeans. Abbie was wearing jeans. When the front door opened and Donny was standing there, he was wearing jeans. I looked down at my good skirt and blouse. It was too late to change.

Right about then my bratty brother almost knocked Donny over by cruising through the door on a skateboard.

"Christopher, not in the house. And do you think that's wise with your broken hand?" my dad said.

Chris didn't answer. He just circled the room, making a road map on the light-colored carpet. Finally Chris stopped because no one was paying any attention to him. But they were paying a lot of attention to Donny. He sure looked cute.

"So, Donny," my dad asked, "how are you doing in school?"

"Not too good."

"So, Donny," my dad asked again, "what does your father do?"

"Oh, he's out of work right now."

I was so embarrassed I wanted to shrivel up and die. I was standing up holding a dish towel, and there was no place to sit on the couch. I could sit on a chair across the room, but talk about feeling left out.

Grandma tiptoed softly in and said, "I don't want to intrude, but dinner is ready, so everybody should sit down." We all sat. Donny sat opposite me. Abbie had managed to sit next to him. Grandma put out the juicy roast beef, the plate of baked potatoes, a huge salad bowl, and a little plate of pickles and olives. Then she ran back into the kitchen.

My father threw his napkin on his plate and said firmly, "Oh, no, she doesn't," and he followed her into the kitchen.

I made a face. Daddy knew that she didn't like to eat with everybody when she had cooked. She preferred to nibble alone in the kitchen. Everyone could hear them arguing. My face turned red when we heard my dad say, "Mother, you are not the maid!"

Donny whispered, "Is your mother living?"

"She's working tonight," I said.

My dad came back without my grandma. Actually I think she had the best idea. Chris has this obnoxious habit of kicking his legs when he's eating and annoying all of us. He was sitting next to me, and I raised my hand to punch him so he'd stop. To my horror, I accidentally knocked over the glass of V-8 juice my grandma had put by each plate. Before I could right it the juice was creeping all over the delicate white tablecloth, spreading like blood.

Almost as if she had eyes in the back of her head, my grandma came charging into the room with sponges and paper towels. Abbie put on her big sister tone of voice and said, "Really, Betsi, can't you be more careful?" Maybe she regretted it after, I don't know, but I did know I wanted to die on the spot. Donny shifted in his chair uncomfortably.

I sat rigidly silent, chewing my food thirty-two times, while my dad and Abbie talked to Donny. If only I hadn't gotten all dressed up. If only I hadn't spilled that V-8 juice. That was all I could think of. I couldn't think of one thing to say until finally I came up with, "Donny, did you know Chris is a concert pianist?"

"Yeah," he said. "I think someone in school told me that."

I stared at Chris's big white wand of a hand. Why couldn't he have spilled the juice instead of me? I heard someone whisper my name. It was Grandma, hiding in the dining room doorway. "Pssst, Betsi."

I got up and went into the kitchen. "So how's it going? Do we have a steady yet?" she asked.

"Nope, but maybe Abigail does," I said bitterly. "I mean, all she does is talk to him. I understand she has this competitive spirit, but she's too old for him."

"Oh, she's just helping you out," Grandma said. "And now it's time for the chocolate cake. Why don't you carry it out? You'll be the center of attention."

You've never tasted chocolate cake like my grandma makes, and her mocha frosting I think she should patent. So it was special to carry out the cake. I shall never forget carrying that cake as long as I live. Somewhere between the edge of the bumpy carpet and the freshly waxed floor my strapless little heel caught, and as everyone smiled expectantly, I fell across the room, crash-landing on the wool carpet. There was a stunned silence as my dad rushed to help me up and ask if I was all right. I assured him I was, moved away, humiliated, and stepped right in the chocolate cake.

What could go wrong? my mom had asked. Everything!

Grandma rushed out with more sponges and paper towels and said cheerfully, "There's ice cream in the freezer."

"Yeah, but it's vanilla," Chris said.

I felt in that instant as if I'd been blinded and struck deaf. I was in shock. Grandma lifted my foot and wiped the frosting off my shoe. Then she disappeared and brought out these big dessert plates with little lumps of white ice cream so it would go around. She dotted each plate with chocolate chip cookies from a supermarket box and prodded me. "Sit down. Go ahead. You'll be fine. It was an accident."

I stumbled into my chair, almost missing it, and closed my eyes. After dessert Donny said, "I want to thank you very much for having me to dinner, but now I have to go home and do my homework."

"Come again, Donny," my dad said. "Next time Mrs. Paulson will be here." Oh, thank God he didn't say, "And we'll all have chocolate cake."

I got up to walk him to the door, and I was surprised that Abigail didn't beat me to it. Now what was I supposed to say? I hadn't really said anything to him all night. Tammy had said he liked me. Maybe there was a chance. In a funny way maybe he liked me. I looked down, and there was still some creamy frosting clinging to my panty hose. I had to stop my urge to bend over and flick it off.

Donny stopped at the door and turned. "It was really nice of you to invite me, Betsi. It's been lonely with my mom away. And my dad just likes stuff like warmed-over pizza, or chili out of a can, or sometimes Chinese food. You have a really nice family, and your mother must be nice, too. "Say, did you do your French homework yet? That lesson was really hard," he continued.

Then I swallowed hard. "Listen, Donny, what do you think about going steady?" My heart was pounding, but I had said it.

"Why?" he asked as he studied me.

"Oh." I shrugged. "I don't know. Just thought I'd ask. I might write a paper about going steady." This was turning out terrible. Why didn't I just come out with it?

"I wanted to ask you if you wanted to go steady with me." There, it was out. I said it.

He tilted my chin upward and smiled down at me. "If I didn't like older girls, I would like you. You're funny and cute, and I wanted to laugh when you dropped that whole chocolate cake, but I thought you would feel hurt. I do like you, Betsi Paulson, but I can't go steady with you because I'm going with Felicity Grimes.''

I stood staring at the door long after he closed it. Felicity was in the eighth grade. Why hadn't I believed Abbie when she told me? Maybe she was becoming more human.

But I was less human. Everything was lost. Everything was over. I hadn't made it.

Time. I needed more time. Maybe my mother could mail back my birth certificate and ask for an extension.

Grandma excused me from doing the dishes so I could call the Double A's and tell them the bad news. Donny liked older girls. We all goofed. No one figured it out.

Dear Diary,

Two days to twelve. Day Ten.

Diary, my chances look slim. Real slim.
When I'm twelve I'll be the same as I've been at eleven—boring! Chris will have his Carnegie Hall concert. Abbie is getting more A+'s to balance out the unmentionable grade in sewing.

But Diary, I could have been special. I could have been going steady with Donny Delbert, except he likes older girls more.

I'm just Betsi with an *i*. Maybe I can change my name one day.

What can happen now?

Nothing, that's what.

It was a mushy chocolate cake day. I would give it an X+, but D- somehow sounds much worse.

Love and xxx's
Betsi with an *i*

Chapter

TWELVE

I first noticed the new boy a couple of days earlier because he sat right in front of me. His name started with a P, too, but I didn't get a really good look at him until later. I would hate to be a new kid in Morgan School. It took a while before anyone accepted you.

Why was I thinking about him right then? Because he must live near Tammy. I had just seen him jogging around the park. I was almost late to another emergency Saturday meeting.

"Donny likes older girls," I said sadly to Kelly. "He likes older girls," I said again.

Kelly shook her head and said nothing.

Lisa and Lida shook their heads, still not believing it.

Tammy ripped some paper out of her notebook. "Okay, we need a new plan."

127

Lida and Lisa were still looking down. Kelly was shaking her head as if to say, "Enough."

Tammy looked at me sympathetically. "We think we should move on to something else. I mean, we think you should, uh, change, but why can't you be special when you're twelve? There's just not enough time left now."

"Yeah," Kelly said. "We have more important business. Like I think we should change the name of the club."

Everyone stared at her. Did her bra size change to an A? Kelly blushed. "It's just that the name sounds like a dude ranch."

I couldn't believe it. This was supposed to be an emergency meeting about me. I looked around the room, and it was as if I wasn't even in it. I felt like bursting into tears.

"Well," Lisa said, "I like the name."

"Yes," Lida agreed. "We're known by that name."

What about Donny? What about my plans to be special? I felt myself turning invisible. Like I did at home when Chris and Abigail just talked and talked and I had nothing to say. I felt swallowed up.

"Betsi, what do you think?"

"Oh, I like the name we have," I said nonchalantly. But I wasn't nonchalant inside. They had promised me I would be twelve with a bang, and now I was going to do it with a whisper. I guess I accepted it right then. What was I hoping for, a reprieve? They were right. We put all this effort into Donny, and Donny didn't want me. I thought the Double A's were invincible, and when I didn't make it they just dumped me. But I couldn't say anything. I felt like crying, but it was all locked up inside me. Maybe later I would.

Then the meeting was over. I ran down the street alone. Lisa and Lida had something to do. Kelly had to go shopping with her mother.

I guess I wasn't really listening, but from somewhere I heard a voice yell, "Hey, wait up." It was some boy.

"Hey," he said, jogging to catch up with me. "Do I have bad breath or something?"

I stared at him a minute before I recognized him. It was the new boy—P for Paterson—who sat in front of me. He didn't look any happier than I felt. Really, the last thing I wanted was company. I didn't want to make conversation or make him feel better. He was cute, though. In any other school he would have been automatically accepted. But Morgan just wasn't like that.

"Well, it takes a while to get accepted, you know," I said.

"Gee, that's the nicest thing anyone has said to me all day." It was his eyes that pulled me in. They were as blue as his shiny jacket that said Dodgers. "Listen, I know you're Betsi Paulson, and my name is Joey Paterson. My dad gave me five dollars this morning. Can I buy you a slice of pizza or something? Okay?"

I felt like saying I would be a miserable person to have along, but I decided he'd misinterpret it. I couldn't be nasty to him—the poor kid had had enough. I found myself smiling and saying "yes" even though I just wanted to be alone to suffer. There was something about this boy I couldn't say "no" to.

"Why do they exclude new kids?" he asked me while we were walking. "I've been to a lot of schools, because my dad changes jobs a lot, but Morgan is the snootiest."

I shrugged. We were on Broadway now. "It's not really that snooty. Give it some time. Do you do something different?"

He shook his head. "No, not really. My grades are so-so. I'm not that good at sports. I don't play a musical instrument. Nah. Nothing. And you?"

I smiled at him. I thought I would never smile again. "Well, I have a brainy older sister with taffy-colored hair who gets all As, except she got a C minus in sewing. Now she gets A pluses to make up for it. I have a brother who's a musical prodigy. He broke his hand, but it will probably heal better than ever. He's supposed to give a recital at Carnegie Hall. I'm not anything—special."

130

We were facing the front of the pizza parlor when he stopped and said, "You seem pretty popular in school."

"But that's not special. That's just pretty popular in school. So what?"

He shrugged, and I noticed our shrugs were a lot alike. We went into Angela's Pizzeria, and I ordered a broccoli and onion slice, and he ordered a sausage and pepper slice. We had Cokes, and when he paid the man with the five-dollar bill I couldn't help thinking that it looked like we were on a date. But he didn't really ask me out. We just kind of bumped into each other—accidentally. Besides, I'd never been on a date, just at a party.

"My mom died," he said suddenly. "That's why we moved to New York. I'm living with my grandma."

"Oh, I'm sorry to hear that. I have a grandma, too. She's wonderful. She lives upstairs from us. She moved in a little after us. My dad wanted her to have a nice place to live in after my grandpa died."

He was eating the gooey triangle of his pizza when he said, "It must be rough being a middle child, let alone being up against two spoiled-brat geniuses."

"How did you know they were spoiled brats?" Was I really eating and chewing and swallowing in front of someone of the opposite sex?

"How did you know they were spoiled brats?" I asked again, interested.

"Oh, they'd have to be temperamental. Don't forget, I come from California. There are a lot of people like that."

"Can you get a slice in California?" I asked him.

He rolled his eyeballs upward. "You can get everything in California. Sunshine. Swimming. I miss it. I hate New York City."

It felt really comfortable to be with another genuinely miserable person.

"But do you hate New York because you miss the sunshine or because you can't make friends in school?"

Wait until I told my grandma about this conversation with a boy. Wait until I told my diary.

"Why don't they like me?" he said, averting his eyes.

"Oh, give us a chance," I said, like I had all the answers. "It's not that no one likes you. They're—well, just private. It takes them a while to get to know new kids, that's all." I didn't want to tell him about the kid from New Jersey who was so unhappy his parents moved back.

"How old are you?" he asked. Joey was funny. He asked any old question at any old time.

"I'll be twelve tomorrow."

"Happy birthday!"

"No, no, it isn't," I said sadly. "It's just a birthday. I wanted to be special by the time I was twelve. I tried everything. Modeling. Baking special brownies. And then I tried—"

"Tried what?"

Oh, gimme a break. I could never tell that to a boy! But there I was doing it anyway.

"Well, I wanted to go steady with this boy Donny. My club, the Double A's, decided that would make me special. But it didn't work."

"Why not?"

"Oh, he—it—was nothing."

"Oh, it must have been something. Didn't he like you?"

"Oh, no, he said he did. But he likes older girls."

Joey nodded and crunched on the crust of his pizza. Then he jumped up and said, "What about another Coke? I have a dynamite idea." I nodded, and he came back slowly, afraid of spilling the two glasses.

There was something I liked about Joey, but I wasn't sure what. Of course, I would always like Donny. That was a different kind of like. But there was something odd about Joey. I felt comfortable with him.

He sucked on his straw and then stared me in the eye. "I see an opportunity for a trade-off," he said thoughtfully.

I looked up.

"You're going to be twelve, and you feel you didn't make it. You think you're not special."

I nodded.

"I want to be popular, and I can't unless I'm special, but there's nothing especially special I do. You see?"

I didn't.

"So let's go steady."

My mouth dropped open, and the straw slid out of my mouth. I didn't like him *that* way. But—

"Look, I can even give you something to show that we go together." He reached inside his pants pocket and pulled out a ring with a turquoise stone. "It was my mother's," he said solemnly. "I carry it around for good luck. Now *she* was special."

I looked at the ring, thinking I couldn't take it.

"Don't you like me?" he said, and for the first time I thought he was a little shy.

I did. I liked him a lot, but it wasn't the same as love. He was one of the friendliest, most honest boys I had ever met. It was a shame that none of the kids at Morgan knew how great he was.

I smiled at him and tried on the ring. It fit perfectly, and it was beautiful.

"Okay," he said, shaking my hand. "It's a deal. Now it's Betsi and Joey or Paterson and Paulson."

"Paulson and Paterson," I corrected him, unable to stop grinning.

"Now your sister will have a chance to be green with envy, and your little brother will be jealous, too. They have trouble making friends."

"Do you think so?" I looked around the pizzeria and saw some kids I knew from another school come in. They were staring at us.

"Oh, sure. They must. They've got to be totally self-absorbed."

Wait until I told the Double A's. They'd be thrilled for me! Joey was great! Of course, he wasn't Donny, but I couldn't even talk to Donny. This was, after all, a business deal.

"Now that you're wearing my mom's ring, let me tell you a little bit about her. She was a painter. And she would have told you it was nice you have a boyfriend, but you should also have a career."

"Your mother told you that?"

"Well, she would have told *you* that. I have to have a career. I'm going to go into sales, just like my dad."

I thought he had made a great beginning.

"Your mom sure must have been nice, Joey," I said.

"Yeah. I would still be in California if not for . . ." His voice kind of broke, but then he became cheerful. "Now you'll be going steady by the time you're twelve, and that's what you wanted." He was smiling at me.

I looked at the ring and waited for the automatic butterflies that came when I had a crush on someone. But they didn't happen. However, I did feel comfortable.

"You have a little piece of pizza on your chin," Joey said, and he took a napkin and dabbed it off. For a second I thought I'd crawl under the pizza booth. He was smiling. I loved his smile. Trouble was, no one had ever seen it because he never smiled in school.

There was one person who would love this. Boy, would she love this. Joey was the kind of boy you brought home to your grandma.

We got up to leave, and for some reason I noticed that he was about two heads taller than me. I liked that. Donny was about the same height.

We stopped at the door, and he looked down at me.

"Betsi, I have to be honest. I know this is a good deal for both of us, but I also like you a lot."

Dear Diary,

Day Eleven. One day more to twelve.

I made it, Di. I'll be going steady by the time I'm twelve, and it's going to create a sensation. But with a different boy. Not with Donny. My steady is this new boy from Los Angeles, California.

Oh, Di, it's so romantic. Wait until the girls hear. I just know we'll do all the things people who go together do. Go to the movies, hold hands, do homework together, have people be jealous of us.

Unfortunately, no one will know until Monday in school,

because my birthday's on Sunday. I hope it doesn't rain. The Double A's are calling another emergency meeting for tomorrow. Grandma will probably make me a powder-blue cake.

Actually I feel like I'm twelve already. Nothing more can happen. I'm going steady with a boy who gave me a turquoise ring.

Today was a turquoise day with a splash of pink hearts and a smidgen of dark purple. This is one of the few days that went from an X all the way to an A.

Chapter
THIRTEEN

Everything has to be perfect on my birthdays. What I eat, what I wear, who I see, my party. Of course this year I wouldn't be having a birthday party, because I was twelve. My mom promised me my own phone. Also she'd take Abbie and me to lunch and a Broadway play next weekend.

I couldn't believe we were having another emergency meeting of the Double A's. I purposely hadn't called anyone to tell them that I had made it. I was actually going steady. I planned to surprise them. I couldn't wait to tell them.

I wore a powder-blue turtleneck over my powder-blue pants, and I put the turquoise ring on my right hand. I ran into the kitchen and decided I wanted cereal for my birthday breakfast. No one was around. Funny, but there were no birthday cards, no packages wrapped with ribbon. Well, it was probably too early. I wondered what my grandma would give me for my birthday. But I couldn't go up there yet.

You couldn't be late to a meeting of the Double A's. It was in our constitution. I didn't intentionally try to be late, but the sun was shining, and it was my birthday, and I was thinking about Joey. But I guess the real reason was who wants to go to an emergency meeting on a Sunday? What was the emergency?

When I finally jogged over to Tammy's apartment I had rehearsed five different ways to tell them I was going steady with Joey. I had made it by my twelfth birthday!

They were all waiting for me in Tammy's bedroom. I held up my turquoise ring, but all Kelly and Tammy said was "You're late."

"We already started," said Lisa.

"It's a crucial meeting," Lida said.

I guessed it was so crucial they would wait until later to wish me a happy birthday.

"Betsi," Tammy said, "we called this meeting to change the name of the club."

"But it's always been the Double A's." No one said anything. "I thought we decided to leave it the way it was."

"Before you got here we were thinking of names. Tulip was one," Kelly said. "It's nice, isn't it?"

"Yeah," I said. "It's pretty. But I like Double A's."

"But it does sound like a dude ranch, and besides, in a year it will be obsolete anyway."

For one second the name change seemed kind of silly to me.

I wanted to tell them the terrific news about Joey, but I just couldn't find an opening.

Kelly said, "Before you got here we proposed taking in a new member."

"A new member? There's no one left to be in a club!" I said. "Who?"

"Cheryl." Cheryl always wore sweaters and jeans and a locket on a chain and socks and sneakers. She wore braces and two long ponytails that stuck out on either side of her head. Cheryl was okay. But her mother didn't approve of girls' clubs and had forbidden her to be in one. Why would we invite Cheryl? She couldn't even come.

"Why would we invite Cheryl in?" I asked.

"Well, she's going to ask her mother again," Lisa said.

Suddenly I, a generally even-tempered person, began to get angry. Something was very funny. The Double A's weren't acting like club sisters to me. They weren't even acting nice to me. So I flashed my turquoise ring and said, "Well, I have something to say. I am going steady. His name is Joey, and we are the first sixth graders to go steady. Look, I have a ring and everything. I made it!"

I didn't realize I had been standing up, so I sat down and waited for their reaction.

Tammy spoke first. "We know."

"We know," Lisa and Lida said together.

"We know," Kelly said.

140

"You know?"

"Well, yes. Joey called me, and I called everybody I knew," Tammy blurted out. "And now everybody knows you're more than Betsi with an i."

"You didn't call any of us," Kelly said, and suddenly I felt like I was on trial.

"But I thought I'd surprise you today and show you the ring he gave me. I thought we could all celebrate together instead of making a bunch of phone calls. But the important thing is I'm going steady and I'm twelve and I'm special." I left out the business deal part of it.

"Yeah," Kelly said, looking down at the rug, "but it's the wrong boy. It's Joey."

"What's wrong with Joey?" I said. "You just have to get to know him. He's cute and he's nice and he's sweet and he's—"

"Not Donny," Tammy finished for me.

"But Donny didn't work. Besides, I couldn't talk to Donny without feeling I had organic peanut butter in my mouth."

"You mean you can really *talk* to Joey?" Kelly asked, but she was almost drowned out by Tammy, who was of course still president of Tulip or Double A.

"But don't you understand, Betsi? Suddenly you spring this surprise. You're going steady with Joey, a new boy nobody even knows. But with Donny—well, we did that together. The Double A's. It was our project. And if he had said yes—"

I quickly reminded her that he had said no and liked older girls.

"Just like that," Kelly said.

"But the point is we would all have been going steady with Donny, and we could have told you what to wear and what he said and what to say back to him.

"But now," Lisa and Lida said, "it's different."

"How different?" I asked.

"You'll see," Tammy said. "It will just be different."

I looked around the room at my very dearest friends in this whole wide world, and little tears formed in my eyes. I was going to be special. I was twelve, and this was the worst birthday I had ever had.

"Well, I nominate Cheryl to be in the club. I talked to her last night, and she said her mother might really change her mind," Tammy said.

"But we've always been five," I protested.

There was silence after I said that, and then something strange happened. Lida began to cry. Then Lisa fell across her twin sister and sobbed all over her identical top. Kelly had problems with crying, so she tied and untied her shoelaces.

Only Tammy wasn't crying. Tammy had problems with being honest sometimes. Finally she said, "Don't you see?"

I didn't.

"You are in the sixth grade. And you have a boyfriend. Not someone we picked out for you so we could all tell you how to do it. You're going steady!"

"But that's good," I protested.

"No, now you have a boyfriend, and you won't have any time for your girlfriends, your dearest friends. It's always that way when girls get boyfriends."

"We feel we're losing a member, so we wanted Cheryl in," Lisa said.

"Boys get in the way, and they break up friendships with girls."

"But you don't even know Joey. He's not like that at all."

"Already you seemed changed, more sophisticated, more sure of yourself," Kelly said tentatively.

"I'll never change. You're my very best friends in the world. And maybe if I seem happy it's because I was unhappy trying to go steady with Donny. At least I can talk to Joey."

I stood up and solemnly swore to be a good and faithful member of the Double A's. Then everyone was crying like they were afraid they were going to lose me or something. Tammy passed around a box of pink Kleenex.

"I swear to always be a Double A!"

"Or Tulip," Lisa said.

And then we voted to keep it Double A because that's what it was and that's who we were. And I guessed Cheryl wouldn't be in it because her mother really didn't want her to be. It was great. We all took the elevator down together, singing songs and linking arms. Then everyone went home. It was only later that I remembered that no one had sung me "Happy Birthday!"

Oh, well, with all that was going on they had probably forgotten.

When I got home the doorman handed me a huge folded yellow note, and I knew there was one person in the world who would never forget my birthday, and I was right.

Betsi, darling,

Happy birthday. You're twelve. So come up and see the happy birthday surprise Grandma has for you. And remember how special you are. Remember what Grandma always says—the middle part of the sandwich is best. So wouldn't you rather be a slice of salami or cheese or peanut and jelly between two slices of bread?

I loved the way Grandma put things. After racing down her hall I buzzed our special signal. I wondered what color sweater she had knitted me for my birthday. I couldn't think of any color I didn't already have. Grandma was really a Smart Cookie because whenever I wore one I was a walking ad for her.

I rang my signal and the door was flung open, and Grandma hugged me and pinched my lips until they were oblong, and then she gave me a big, smacking kiss, dragging me inside and shutting the door.

She immediately sat me down on a chair and plunked a big white box tied with bright peach ribbon on my lap.

144

I bet this year's sweater would be peach. I already had five, but when I lifted the top off there was something different in the box.

"Brownies! Grandma, you didn't!" Somehow she had figured out a recipe. There were layers of almost luminous peach-colored brownies like the old strawberry brownies. They were amazing!

"Now, Betsi, you can be special."

"But, Grandma, I am already. I don't have time to be a biz-whiz-kid. I'm going steady. I did it!"

Grandma clasped her hands together. "He had a change of heart. Oh, smart boy."

"No, I changed boys, Grandma. His name is Joey, and he's new to Morgan. No one's been nice to him yet. He wanted to be popular, and I wanted to go steady by the time I was twelve, so we made a deal!"

"But you also like him, Betsi. He's a nice boy?"

"Oh, yes, Grandma. I like him a lot. I like him even better than the boy who was supposed to be my steady."

Grandma pinched my cheeks again until they shook like Jell-O, and then she gave me a big, wet Grandma kiss. "That's my Betsi. You got what you wanted. Come, let's go downstairs and see what's happening."

"But Grandma, aren't you afraid of imposing?"

She shrugged. "Not when it's your birthday."

Our apartment was dark when we got there. Some exciting birthday. No one was even home.

Or that's what I thought.

The lights flashed on, and the whole sixth grade class

from Morgan School sprang out from behind our couch and chairs yelling, "Surprise! Happy Birthday!" My whole family was there, too. Grandma hugged me. Joey came up and kissed me on the cheek. Abigail and Chris came up and hugged me. Abbie said, "I heard about you and Joey. Congratulations." Then she disappeared into the crowd, but I thought she looked kind of sad.

"Who's this boy?" my dad asked. Joey had never left my side, not even when kids were popping all the balloons and when the music started playing and they all started to dance.

"Daddy," I said proudly, "this is Joey. We're going steady!"

I thought he'd be happy, but instead he said in a slightly angry voice, "You have years left to go steady, Betsi. You're only twelve."

All of the Double A's came up and gave me a group hug just then, and Tammy said, "We couldn't wish you a happy birthday this morning because then we would have ruined the surprise party."

My mom rushed up to kiss and hug me. "Quiet, everyone, I have an announcement to make. I don't think a lot of you know it, but Betsi is a very talented writer." I looked around to see if she was really talking about me.

"I just did a writing job, and Betsi helped me with it. She had to name a brand-new china pattern that's white with gold and green trim. She named it Evergreen, and the client bought it. So this check rightly belongs to Betsi."

Everyone watched as she handed me a check.

I sneaked a look at it and almost collapsed. It was for three hundred and fifty dollars. I wondered if I'd have to pay income tax on it. All the kids were crowding around it and me. My head was spinning. My mom had just said I was a talented writer. I always wrote, but I never thought of it as anything special—it was something I just did.

Now I was special, and my writing was special, too.

My dad came up and kissed me. I looked at the check—and at Joey, who was still staring at it with me.

"Daddy, I was special all along, and I didn't even know it."

My dad hugged me. "Betsi, I don't know what you're talking about. You've always been special to us. You're the normal one. You're the kid. Do you know what it's like to have a child prodigy and an all-A student? Sometimes your mom and I just don't know how to handle their kind of specialness. But of course, you're special, too. Even without the check for the plate design you'd be special. Even without that new boy of yours—what's his name?"

"Joey."

"Without any of those things you're still special. I never knew you felt you weren't."

Dear Diary,

Day Twelve. No days to go. Happy Birthday, Betsi! I made it!

(I drew balloons and a birthday cake with candles on the cake.)

Well, I made it, but not like I thought I would. I'm special, and it just kind of happened. I have a boyfriend, and I like him, Di, I really do. The whole sixth grade class knows we're going steady, and that's special.

Of course, Abbie still gets all A's and A pluses and will probably be a nuclear physicist, and Chris's hand is getting better, so he'll probably go from being a pint-size famous pianist to a grown-up one.

But now, Di, I realize I'm not just sandwiched between two dazzling geniuses. I'm special, too.

But I'm saving the best for last. At my surprise party my mother said I was getting paid for being a writer. I'm a professional writer, Di. I named a plate. But I don't just want to name plates, I want to be a real writer.

I'm thinking of writing a story, Dear D., and it's going to be about the most unforgettable character I ever knew.

That's right.

You guessed it.

My grandma. The original Smart Cookie.

How can I describe my birthday? It was a powder-blue cake with pink and white sprinkles. And the only grade I can give it is an A plus.

Love and xxx's
Betsi with an *i*

About the Author

JUDI MILLER loves to write children's books. She teaches "How to Write Children's Books" at the New School of Social Research in New York City. She is also the author of *Ghost in My Soup, Ghost À La Mode,* and *Figuring Boys Out.* She also writes suspense thrillers for adults.

Judi grew up in Cleveland, Ohio, and if she had a younger brother or sister she would have been a middle child.